OUTER DARKNESS™

DARKNESS™

CHEW™

CREATED BY
JOHN LAYMAN
AFU CHAN
ROB GUILLORY

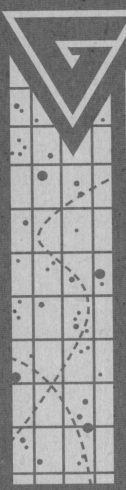

BRIDGE CREW
RANK

608 **JOHN LAYMAN**
CREATOR/WRITER

975 **AFU CHAN**
CREATOR/ARTIST/COVER

734 **ROB GUILLORY**
ARTIST

174 **PAT BROSSEAU**
LETTERER WITH JOHN LAYMAN

922 **JON MOISAN**
EDITOR

CHEW CREATED BY
60734 **JOHN LAYMAN** & **ROB GUILLORY**

52387 **ANDRES JUAREZ** **CARINA**
& **TOM B. LONG** **TAYLOR**
LOGO DESIGN   PRODUCTION DESIGN

FUEL LEVELS

FOR SKYBOUND
ENTERTAINMENT

ROBERT KIRKMAN
Chairman

DAVID ALPERT
CEO

SEAN MACKIEWICZ
SVP, Editor-in-Chief

SHAWN KIRKHAM
SVP, Business Development

BRIAN HUNTINGTON
VP, Online Content

SHAUNA WYNNE
Publicity Director

ANDRES JUAREZ
Art Director

ALEX ANTONE
Senior Editor

JON MOISAN
Editor

ARIELLE BASICH
Associate Editor

CARINA TAYLOR
Graphic Designer

PAUL SHIN
Business Development Manager

JOHNNY O'DELL
Social Media Manager

DAN PETERSEN
Sr. Director of Operations & Events

Foreign Rights Inquiries
ag@sequentialrights.com

Other Licensing Inquiries
contact@skybound.com

SKYBOUND.COM

IMAGE COMICS, INC.

ROBERT KIRKMAN
Chief Operating
Officer

ERIK LARSEN
Chief Financial Officer

TODD McFARLANE
President

MARC SILVESTRI
Chief Executive
Officer

JIM VALENTINO
Vice President

ERIC STEPHENSON
Publisher / Chief
Creative Officer

JEFF BOISON
Director of Sales &
Publishing Planning

KAT SALAZAR
Director of PR &
Marketing

DREW GILL
Cover Editor

HEATHER DOORNINK
Production Director

NICOLE LAPALME
Controller

IMAGECOMICS.COM

FUSION CUISINE

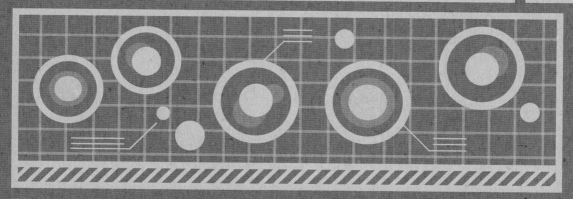

758 >>>_ QUANTUM WARDS ALPHA 37.239753 88.19483 -120.69952 -168.454783 2.1478663 EXORCISM SUCCESSFUL
653 -97.53299 1.16 RESURRECTION FAILED >>>_ NEW ATTEMPT .0349SEC >_ 39.19273 -4.32983 55.435928 9.384758 -46.90415
15.08234 -21.00382 -108.98404 1.15 -22.03528 -2.72653 1.16 ANALYSIS >>>_ .0349SEC >_ -4.32983 55.435928 9.384758 -46.90415 44.61348 -113.23677 34.4598 -45.69123-4.32983 55.435928 9.384758 57.623235 152.07075 3.49 6.69716 -72.84844 1.01 37.66841 -4.32983 55.435928 9.384758 57.623235 152.07075 3.49 6.69716 -72.84844 1.01 37.66841 15.08234 -7.32513 55.435928 9.384758 57.623235 152.07075 3.49 6.69716 -72.32556 1.01 37.66841 15.08234 -21.00382 -108.98404 1.15 -22.03528 -2.72653 1.1 BATTLE AUTHORIZATION >>>_ SUCCESSFUL ATTEMPT .0349SEC >_ -4.32983 55.435928 9.384758 -46.90415 44.61348 -113.23677 -45.69123
-72.84844 1.01 37.66841 15.08234 -21.00382 -108.98404 1.15 -22.03528 -2.72653 1.16 .0349SEC >_ -4.32983 55.435928 9.384758 -46.90415 44.61348 -113.23677 34.4598 -45.69123 55.435928 9.384758 57.623235 152.07075 3.49 6.69716 -72.84844 1.01 37.66841 15.08234 71.393884 3.021 5.73942 -4.32983 55.3554832 9.384758 57.623235 152.0749 6.69716
XR ANALYSIS READOUT

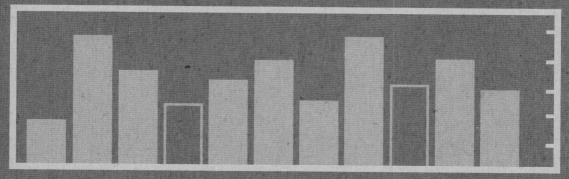

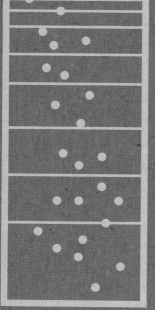

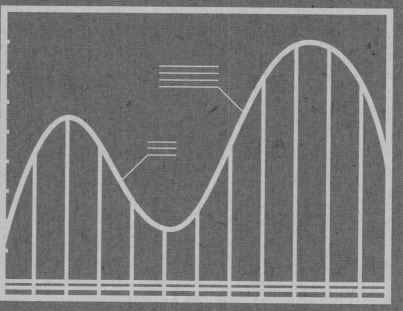

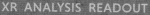

PART 1

FUSION CUISINE

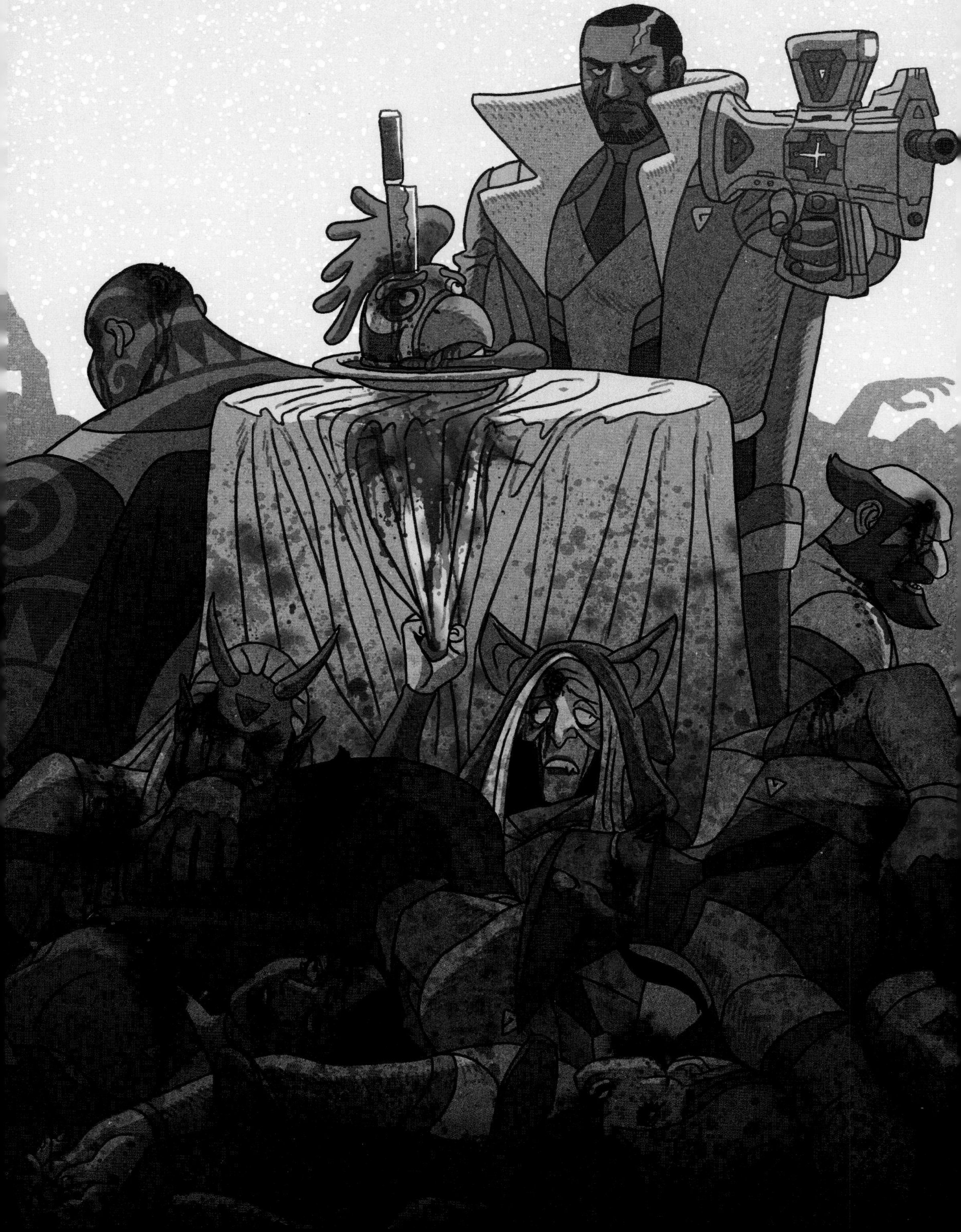

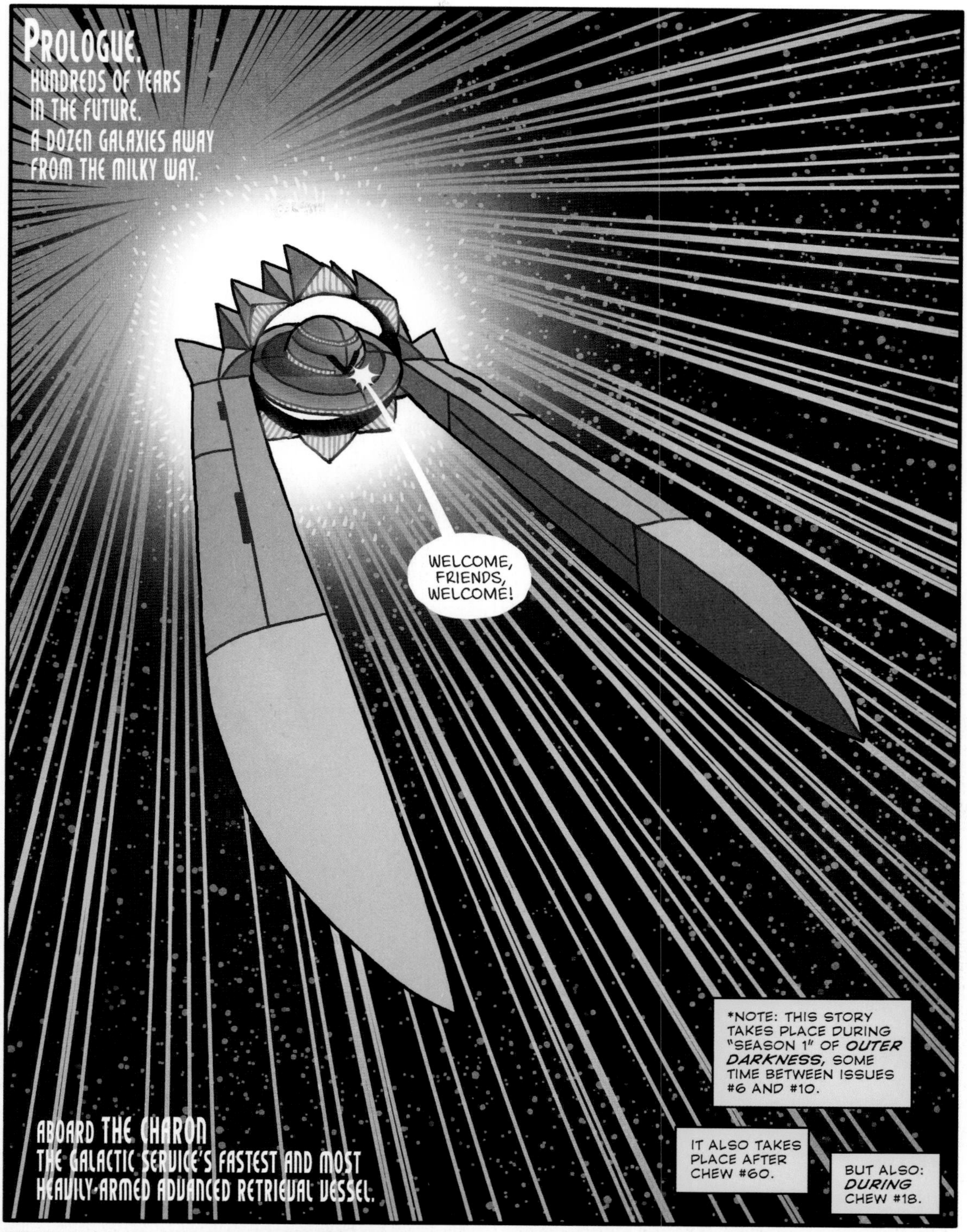
PROLOGUE.
HUNDREDS OF YEARS IN THE FUTURE.
A DOZEN GALAXIES AWAY FROM THE MILKY WAY.
WELCOME, FRIENDS, WELCOME!
*NOTE: THIS STORY TAKES PLACE DURING "SEASON 1" OF OUTER DARKNESS, SOME TIME BETWEEN ISSUES #6 AND #10.
IT ALSO TAKES PLACE AFTER CHEW #60.
BUT ALSO: DURING CHEW #18.
ABOARD THE CHARON
THE GALACTIC SERVICE'S FASTEST AND MOST HEAVILY-ARMED ADVANCED RETRIEVAL VESSEL.

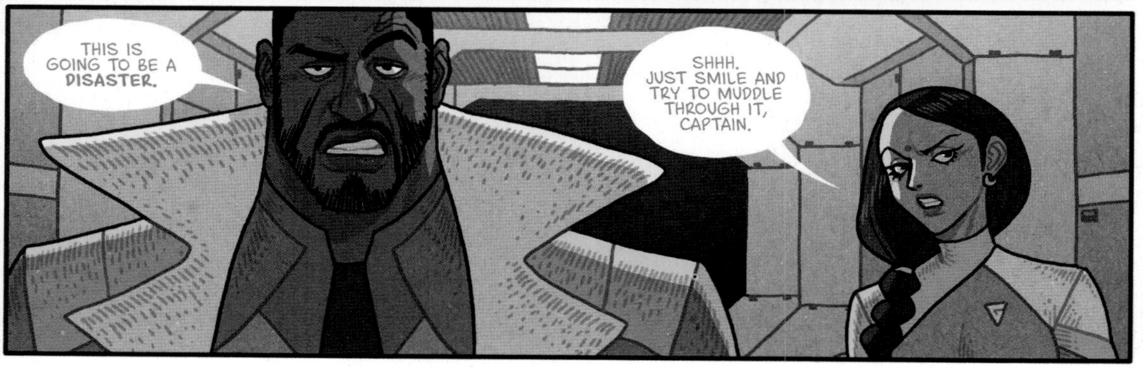
THIS IS GOING TO BE A DISASTER.
SHHH. JUST SMILE AND TRY TO MUDDLE THROUGH IT, CAPTAIN.

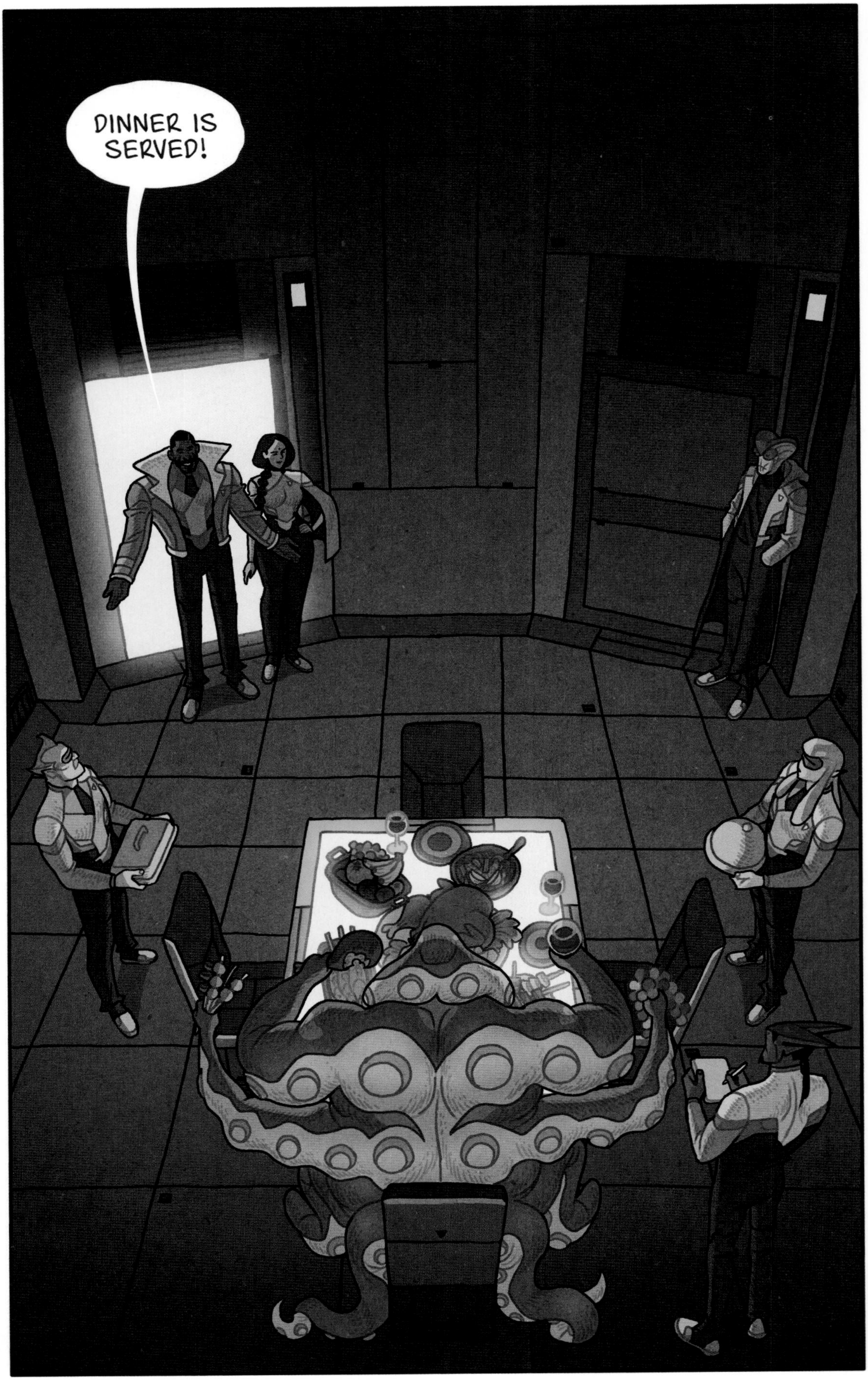
DINNER IS SERVED!

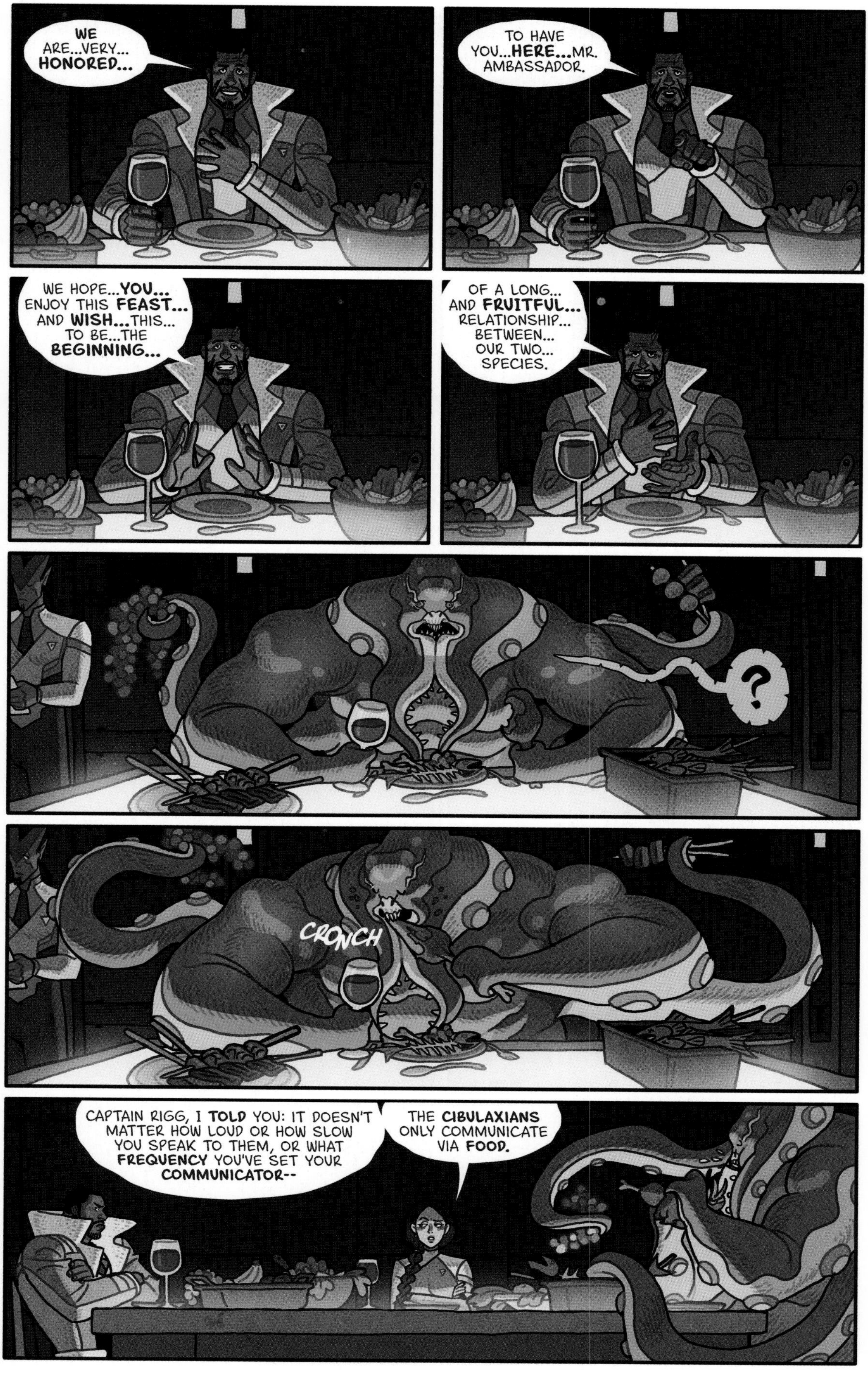

WE ARE...VERY... HONORED...
TO HAVE YOU...HERE...MR. AMBASSADOR.
WE HOPE...YOU... ENJOY THIS FEAST... AND WISH...THIS... TO BE...THE BEGINNING...
OF A LONG... AND FRUITFUL... RELATIONSHIP... BETWEEN... OUR TWO... SPECIES.
?
CRONCH
CAPTAIN RIGG, I TOLD YOU: IT DOESN'T MATTER HOW LOUD OR HOW SLOW YOU SPEAK TO THEM, OR WHAT FREQUENCY YOU'VE SET YOUR COMMUNICATOR--
THE CIBULAXIANS ONLY COMMUNICATE VIA FOOD.

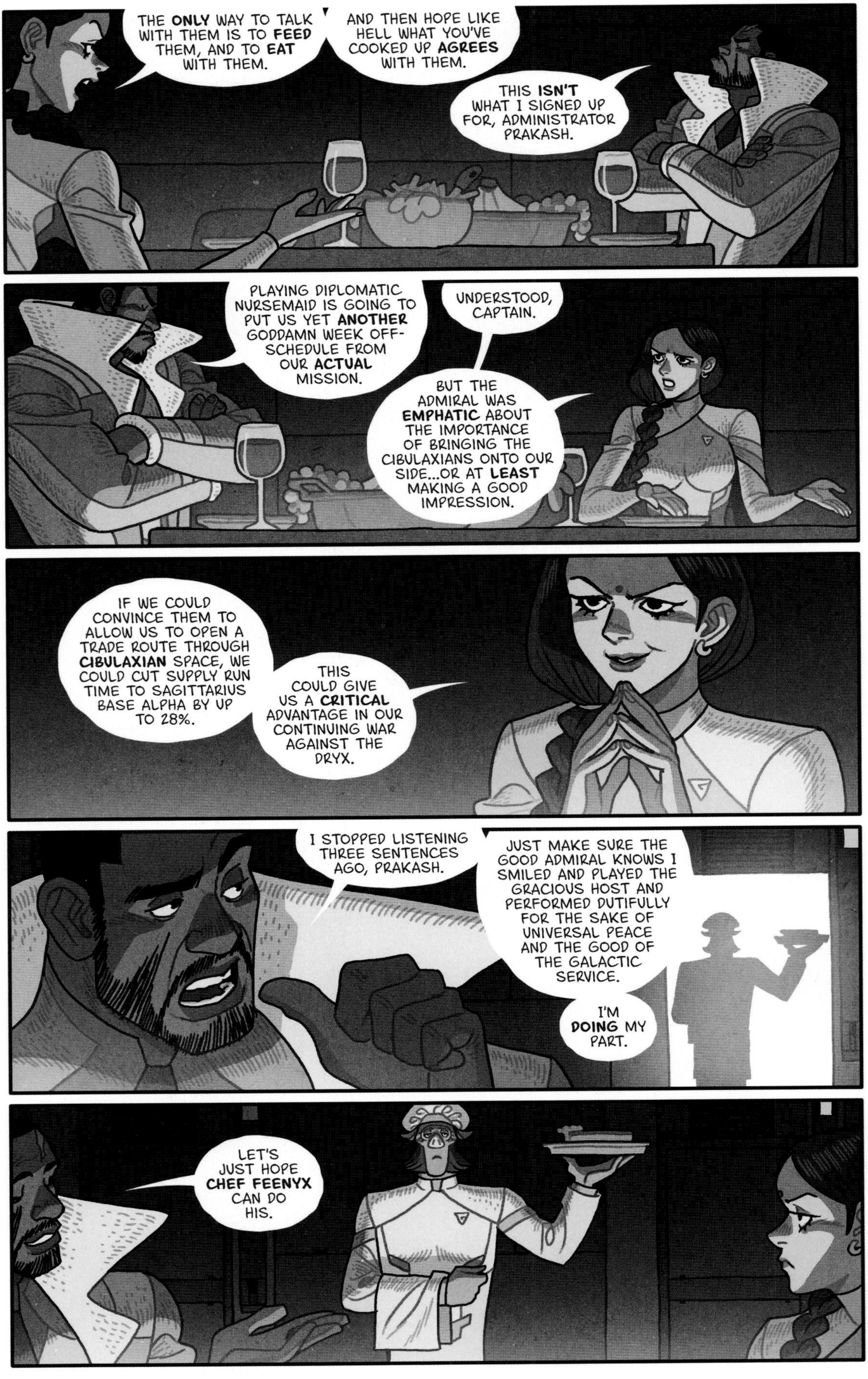
THE ONLY WAY TO TALK WITH THEM IS TO FEED THEM, AND TO EAT WITH THEM.
AND THEN HOPE LIKE HELL WHAT YOU'VE COOKED UP AGREES WITH THEM.
THIS ISN'T WHAT I SIGNED UP FOR, ADMINISTRATOR PRAKASH.
PLAYING DIPLOMATIC NURSEMAID IS GOING TO PUT US YET ANOTHER GODDAMN WEEK OFF-SCHEDULE FROM OUR ACTUAL MISSION.
UNDERSTOOD, CAPTAIN.
BUT THE ADMIRAL WAS EMPHATIC ABOUT THE IMPORTANCE OF BRINGING THE CIBULAXIANS ONTO OUR SIDE...OR AT LEAST MAKING A GOOD IMPRESSION.
IF WE COULD CONVINCE THEM TO ALLOW US TO OPEN A TRADE ROUTE THROUGH CIBULAXIAN SPACE, WE COULD CUT SUPPLY RUN TIME TO SAGITTARIUS BASE ALPHA BY UP TO 28%.
THIS COULD GIVE US A CRITICAL ADVANTAGE IN OUR CONTINUING WAR AGAINST THE DRYX.
I STOPPED LISTENING THREE SENTENCES AGO, PRAKASH.
JUST MAKE SURE THE GOOD ADMIRAL KNOWS I SMILED AND PLAYED THE GRACIOUS HOST AND PERFORMED DUTIFULLY FOR THE SAKE OF UNIVERSAL PEACE AND THE GOOD OF THE GALACTIC SERVICE.
I'M DOING MY PART.
LET'S JUST HOPE CHEF FEENYX CAN DO HIS.

YOUR MAN AGWE FOUND HIM ON TANTALINE IV, AFTER OUR **LAST** CHEF GOT RIPPED APART BY BUCAVACIAN **BLOOD DEMONS.**
THE ONLY OTHER CHEF **MORE** HIGHLY-RATED THAN FEENYX IS SIX-HUNDRED THOUSAND LIGHT-YEARS AWAY.
OH, AND **HERE'S** A SPECIAL TREAT.
KARTYZYIAN MÖTTÖNEN MOON-PIE, BAKED WITH SLOW-ROASTED GHATHAR AND PHAMBERRIES PLUCKED FROM THE ICY SHORES OF MOHXIMAHT VII.
THE SECRET, THOUGH, IS A LIGHT GLAZE OF TANALYNTIAN GHEE.
THEY CAN'T **UNDERSTAND** YOU, CHEF.
NO, OF COURSE. BUT IT IS ALL PART OF THE **PRESENTATION,** NO?
BON APPÉTIT!
!!
!!!

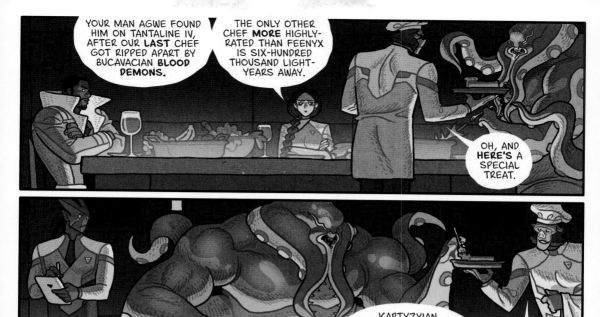

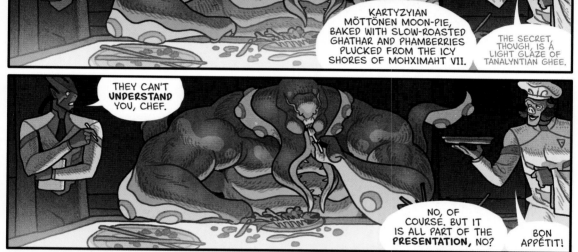

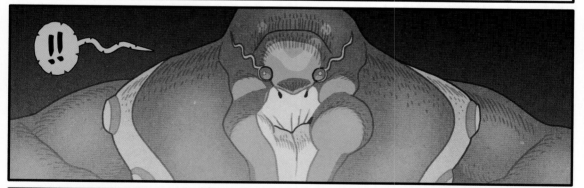

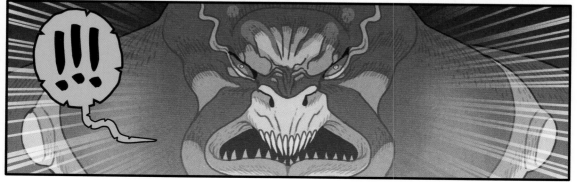

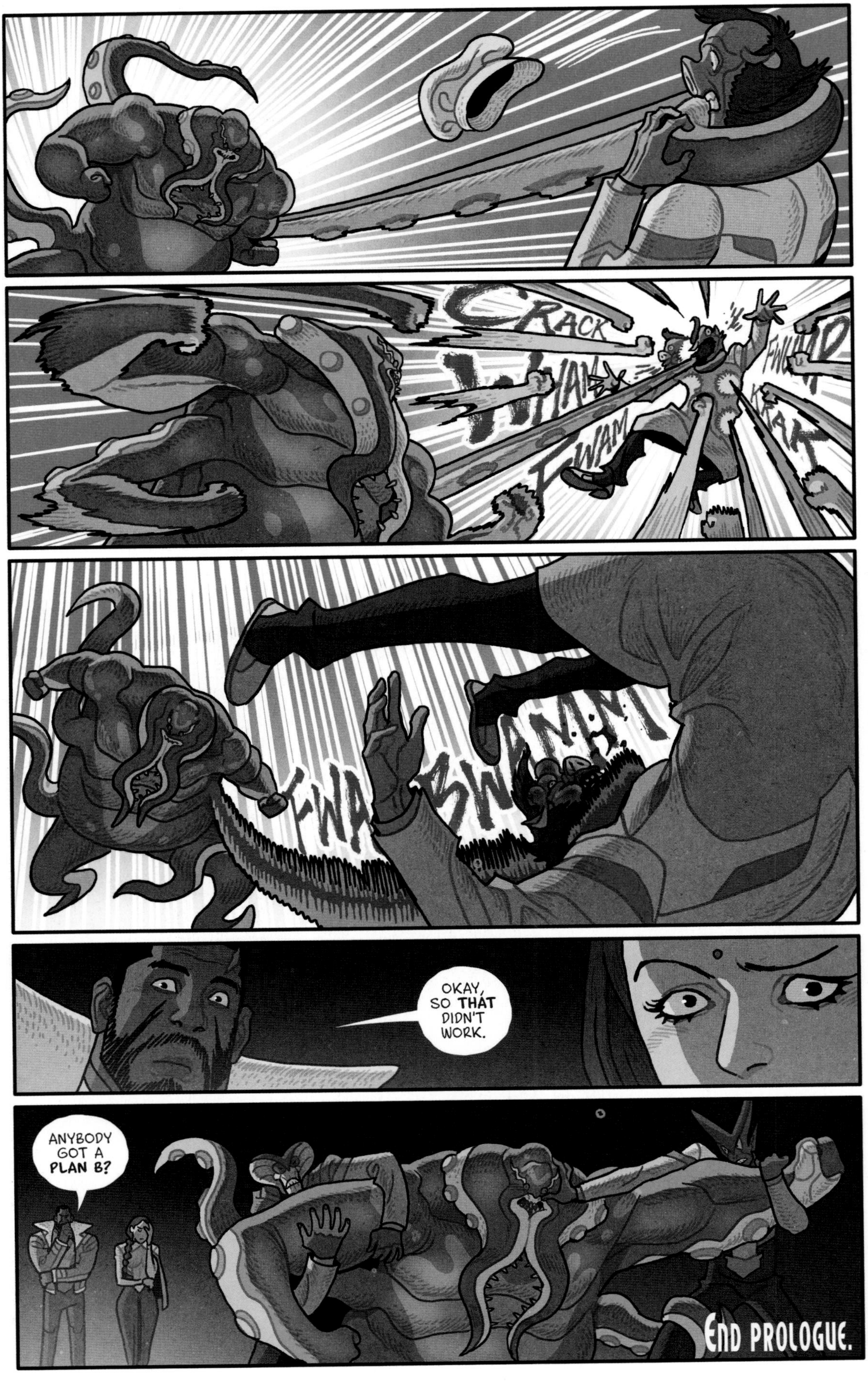
CRACK
FWAM
OKAY, SO **THAT** DIDN'T WORK.
ANYBODY GOT A **PLAN B?**
END PROLOGUE.

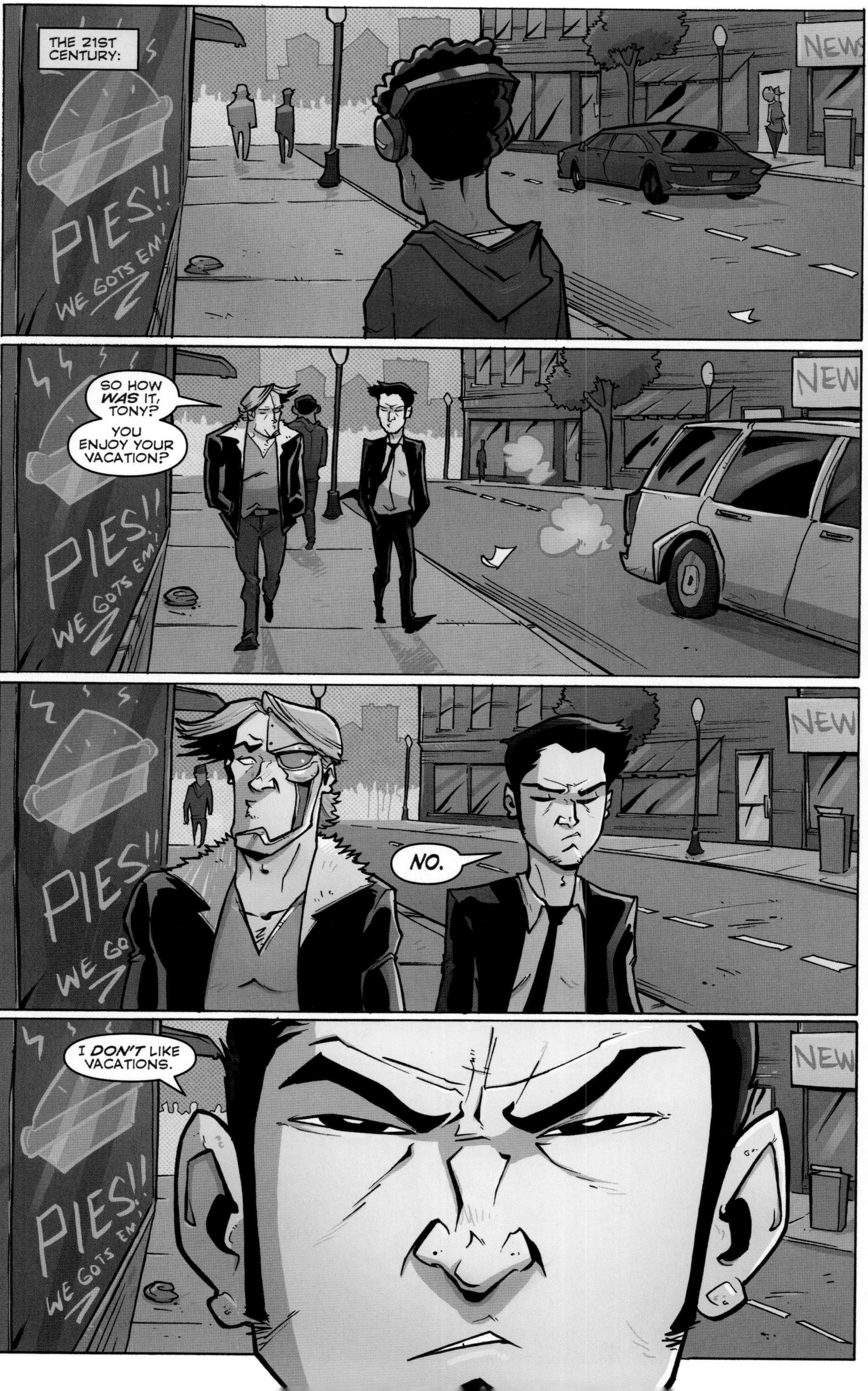
THE 21ST CENTURY:
PIES!! WE GOTS EM!
NEWS
SO HOW WAS IT, TONY?
YOU ENJOY YOUR VACATION?
NO.
I DON'T LIKE VACATIONS.

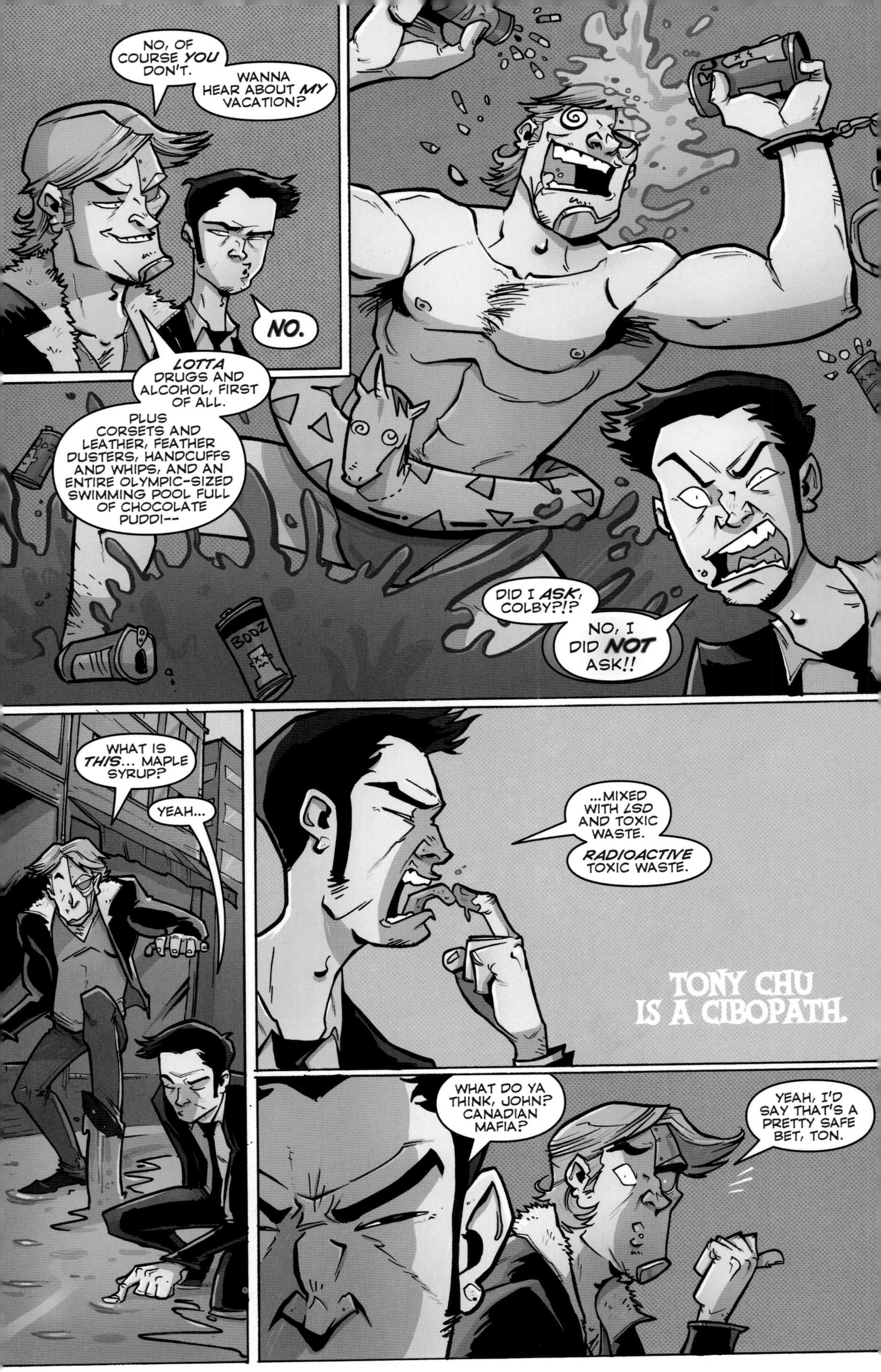
NO, OF COURSE YOU DON'T.
WANNA HEAR ABOUT MY VACATION?
NO.
LOTTA DRUGS AND ALCOHOL, FIRST OF ALL.
PLUS CORSETS AND LEATHER, FEATHER DUSTERS, HANDCUFFS AND WHIPS, AND AN ENTIRE OLYMPIC-SIZED SWIMMING POOL FULL OF CHOCOLATE PUDDI--
BOOZ
DID I ASK, COLBY?!?
NO, I DID NOT ASK!!
WHAT IS THIS... MAPLE SYRUP?
YEAH...
...MIXED WITH LSD AND TOXIC WASTE.
RADIOACTIVE TOXIC WASTE.
TONY CHU IS A CIBOPATH.
WHAT DO YA THINK, JOHN? CANADIAN MAFIA?
YEAH, I'D SAY THAT'S A PRETTY SAFE BET, TON.

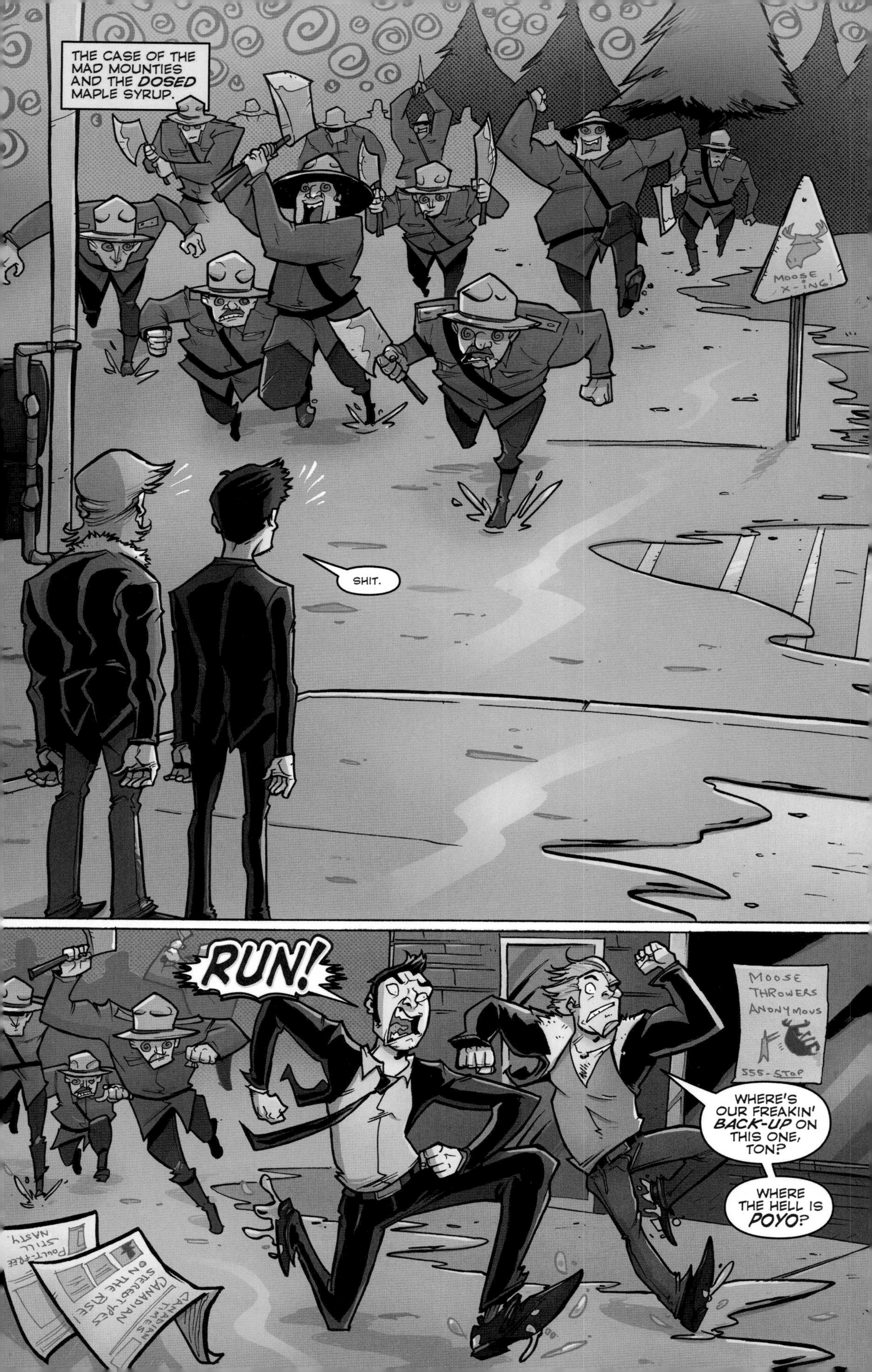
THE CASE OF THE MAD MOUNTIES AND THE DOSED MAPLE SYRUP.
MOOSE X-ING!
SHIT.
RUN!
MOOSE THROWERS ANONYMOUS
555-STOP
WHERE'S OUR FREAKIN' BACK-UP ON THIS ONE, TON?
WHERE THE HELL IS POYO?
CANADIAN TIMES
STEREOTYPES ON THE RISE
POUL-FREE STILL NASTY

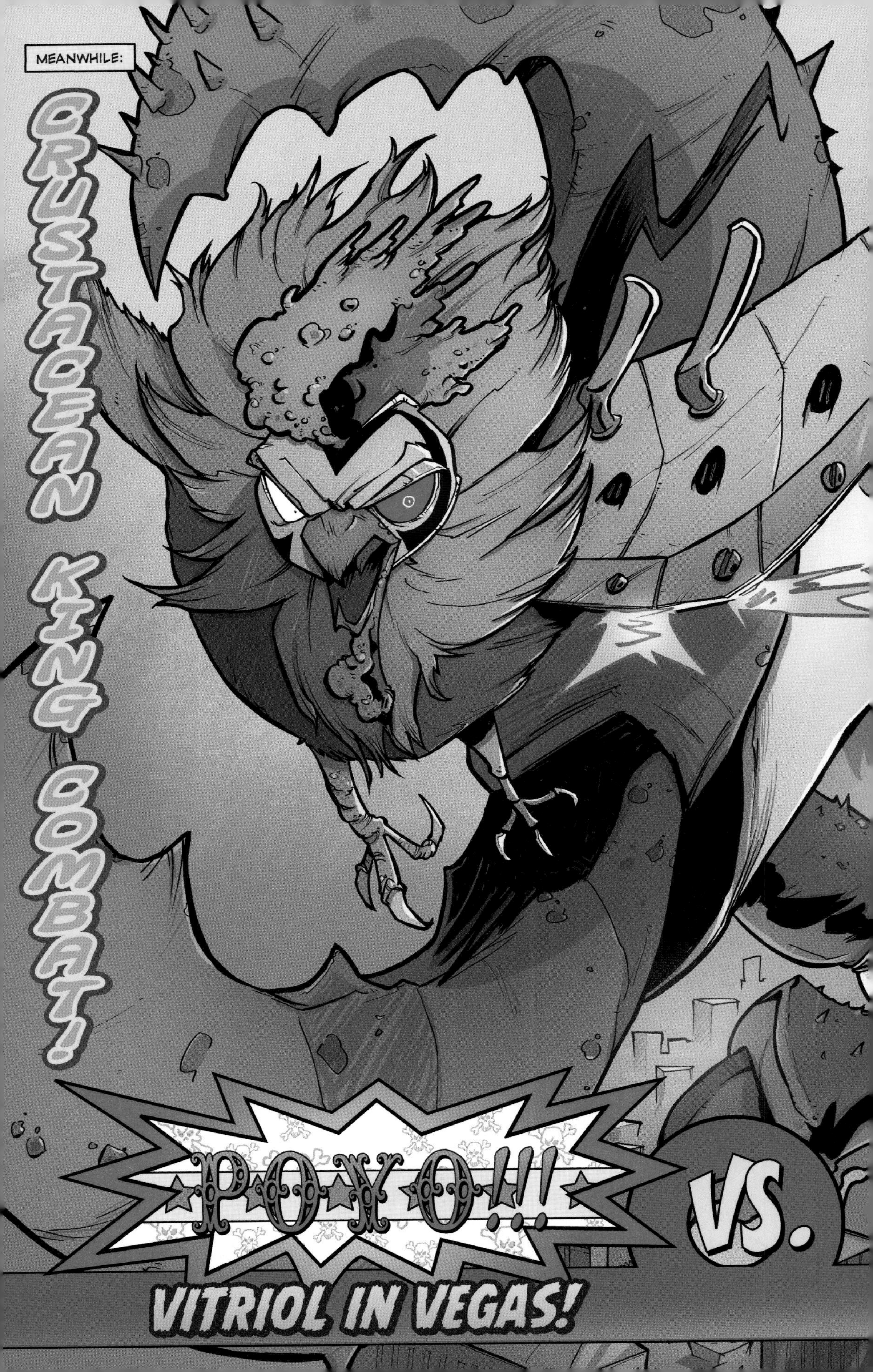
MEANWHILE:
CRUSTACEAN KING COMBAT!
P.O.Y.O!!!
VS.
VITRIOL IN VEGAS!

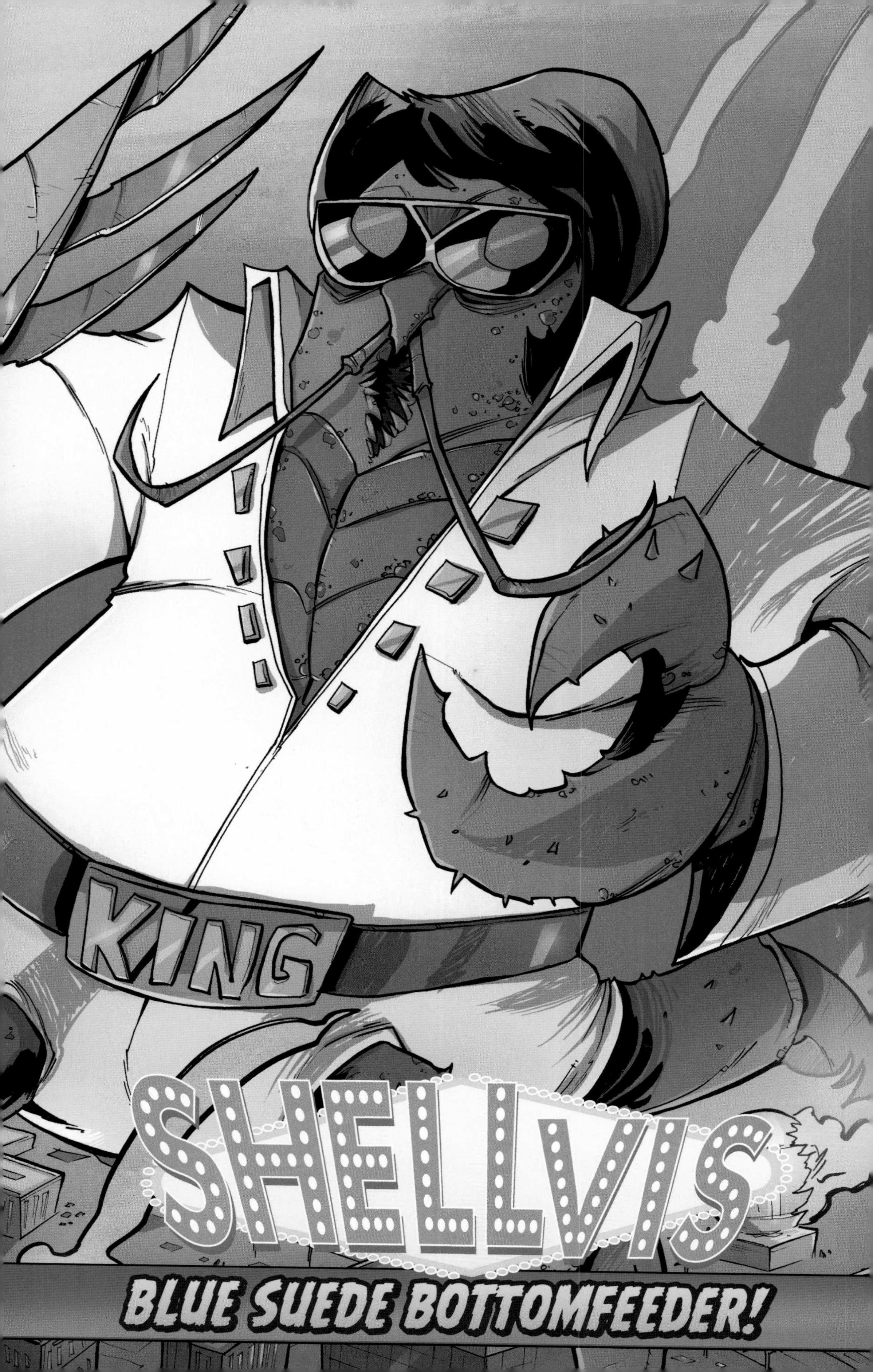
KING
SHELLVIS
BLUE SUEDE BOTTOMFEEDER!

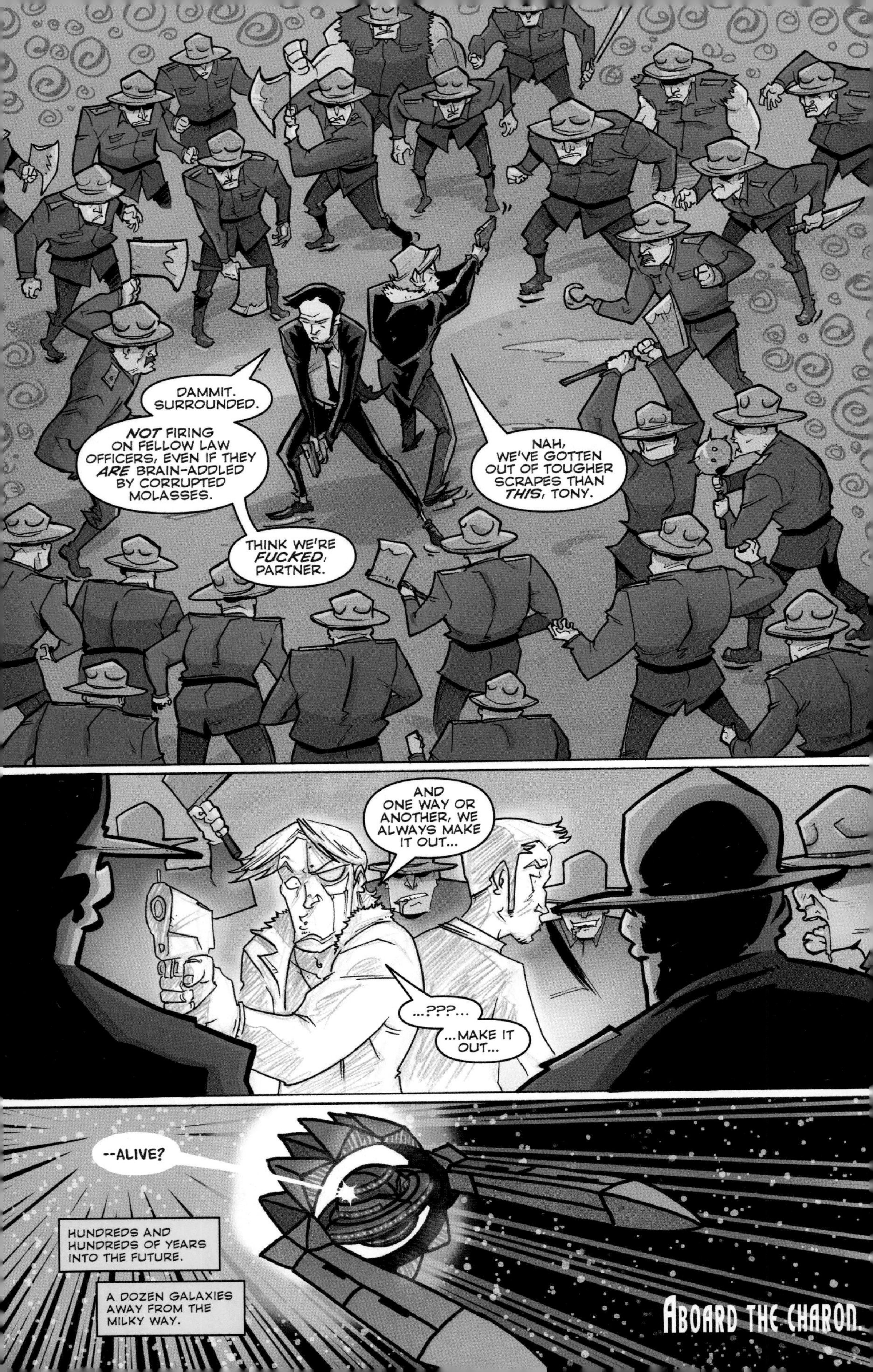
DAMMIT. SURROUNDED.
NOT FIRING ON FELLOW LAW OFFICERS, EVEN IF THEY ARE BRAIN-ADDLED BY CORRUPTED MOLASSES.
THINK WE'RE FUCKED, PARTNER.
NAH, WE'VE GOTTEN OUT OF TOUGHER SCRAPES THAN THIS, TONY.
AND ONE WAY OR ANOTHER, WE ALWAYS MAKE IT OUT...
...???...
...MAKE IT OUT...
--ALIVE?
HUNDREDS AND HUNDREDS OF YEARS INTO THE FUTURE.
A DOZEN GALAXIES AWAY FROM THE MILKY WAY.
ABOARD THE CHARON.

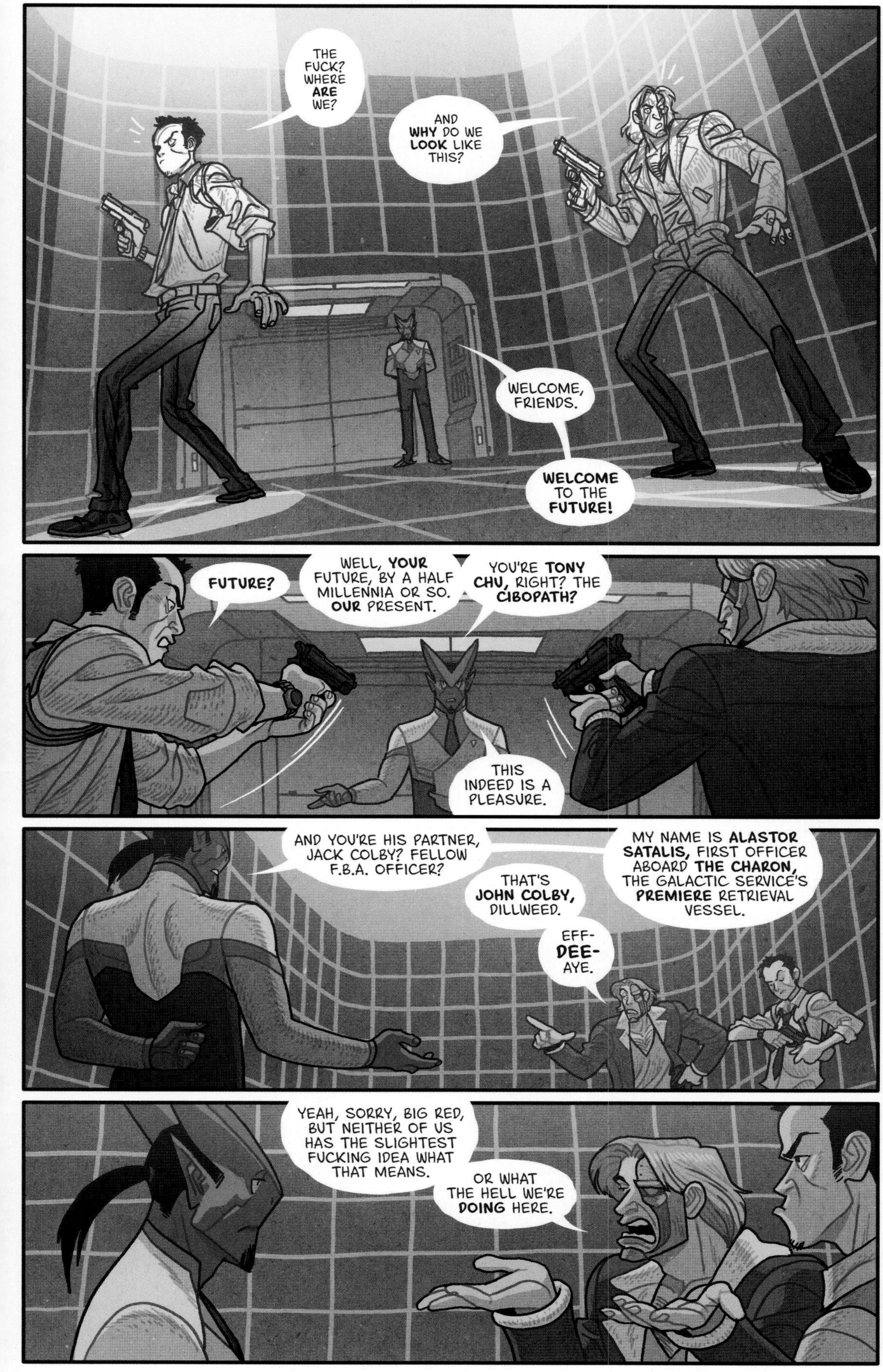
THE FUCK? WHERE ARE WE?
AND WHY DO WE LOOK LIKE THIS?
WELCOME, FRIENDS.
WELCOME TO THE FUTURE!
FUTURE?
WELL, YOUR FUTURE, BY A HALF MILLENNIA OR SO. OUR PRESENT.
YOU'RE TONY CHU, RIGHT? THE CIBOPATH?
THIS INDEED IS A PLEASURE.
AND YOU'RE HIS PARTNER, JACK COLBY? FELLOW F.B.A. OFFICER?
THAT'S JOHN COLBY, DILLWEED.
EFF-DEE-AYE.
MY NAME IS ALASTOR SATALIS, FIRST OFFICER ABOARD THE CHARON, THE GALACTIC SERVICE'S PREMIERE RETRIEVAL VESSEL.
YEAH, SORRY, BIG RED, BUT NEITHER OF US HAS THE SLIGHTEST FUCKING IDEA WHAT THAT MEANS.
OR WHAT THE HELL WE'RE DOING HERE.

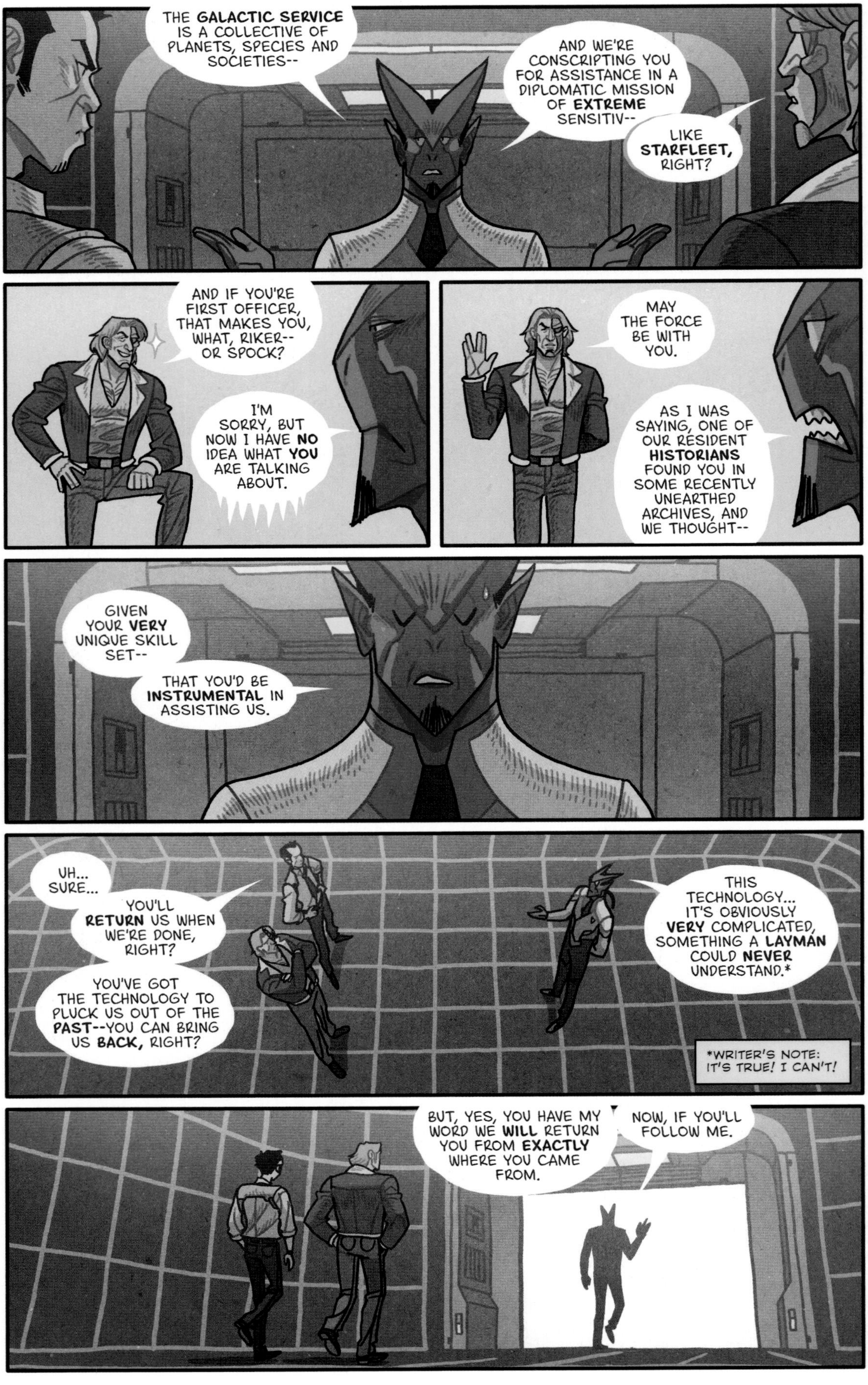
THE GALACTIC SERVICE IS A COLLECTIVE OF PLANETS, SPECIES AND SOCIETIES--
AND WE'RE CONSCRIPTING YOU FOR ASSISTANCE IN A DIPLOMATIC MISSION OF EXTREME SENSITIV--
LIKE STARFLEET, RIGHT?
AND IF YOU'RE FIRST OFFICER, THAT MAKES YOU, WHAT, RIKER-- OR SPOCK?
I'M SORRY, BUT NOW I HAVE NO IDEA WHAT YOU ARE TALKING ABOUT.
MAY THE FORCE BE WITH YOU.
AS I WAS SAYING, ONE OF OUR RESIDENT HISTORIANS FOUND YOU IN SOME RECENTLY UNEARTHED ARCHIVES, AND WE THOUGHT--
GIVEN YOUR VERY UNIQUE SKILL SET--
THAT YOU'D BE INSTRUMENTAL IN ASSISTING US.
UH... SURE...
YOU'LL RETURN US WHEN WE'RE DONE, RIGHT?
YOU'VE GOT THE TECHNOLOGY TO PLUCK US OUT OF THE PAST--YOU CAN BRING US BACK, RIGHT?
THIS TECHNOLOGY... IT'S OBVIOUSLY VERY COMPLICATED, SOMETHING A LAYMAN COULD NEVER UNDERSTAND.*
*WRITER'S NOTE: IT'S TRUE! I CAN'T!
BUT, YES, YOU HAVE MY WORD WE WILL RETURN YOU FROM EXACTLY WHERE YOU CAME FROM.
NOW, IF YOU'LL FOLLOW ME.

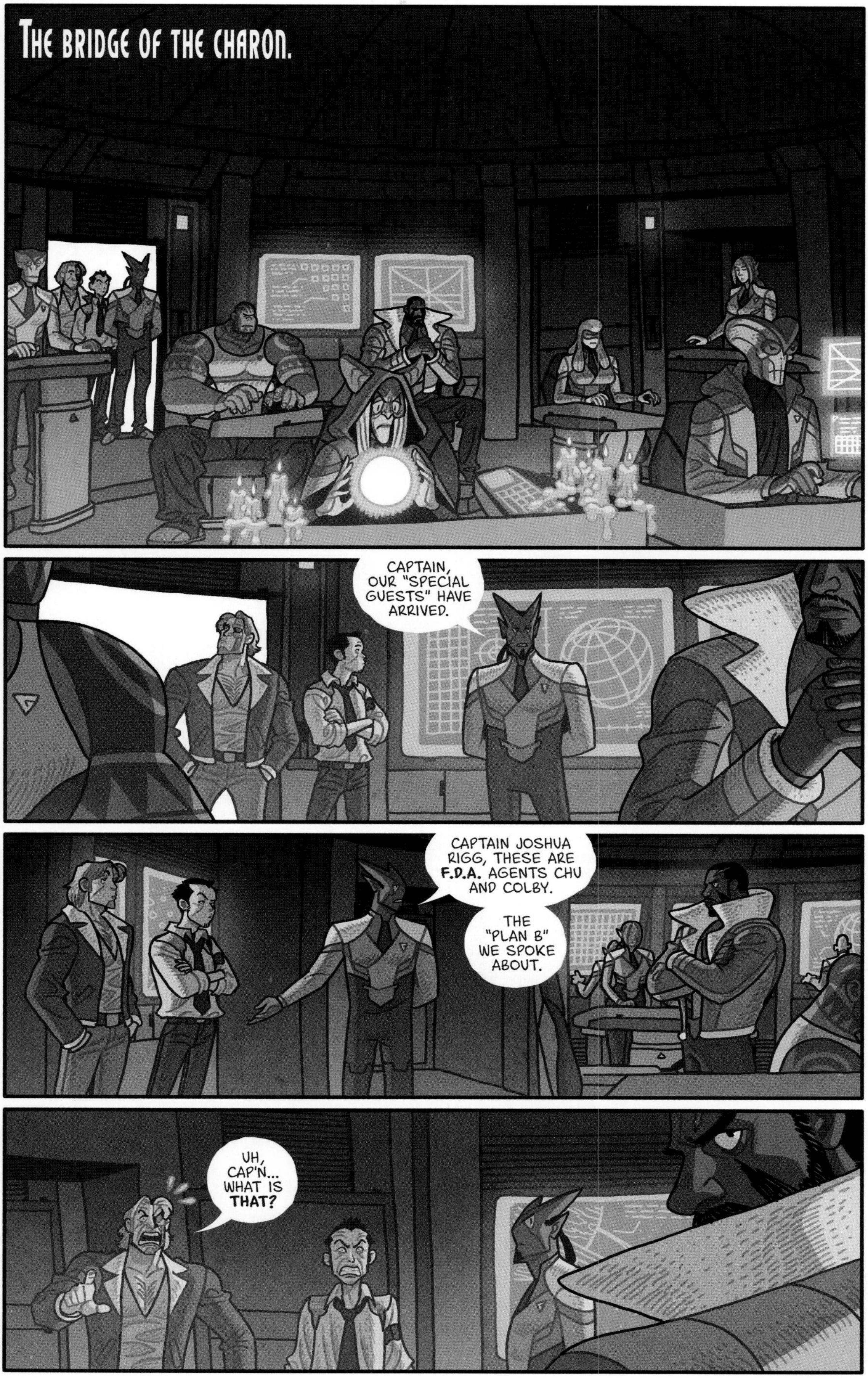
THE BRIDGE OF THE CHARON.
CAPTAIN, OUR "SPECIAL GUESTS" HAVE ARRIVED.
CAPTAIN JOSHUA RIGG, THESE ARE F.D.A. AGENTS CHU AND COLBY.
THE "PLAN B" WE SPOKE ABOUT.
UH, CAP'N... WHAT IS THAT?

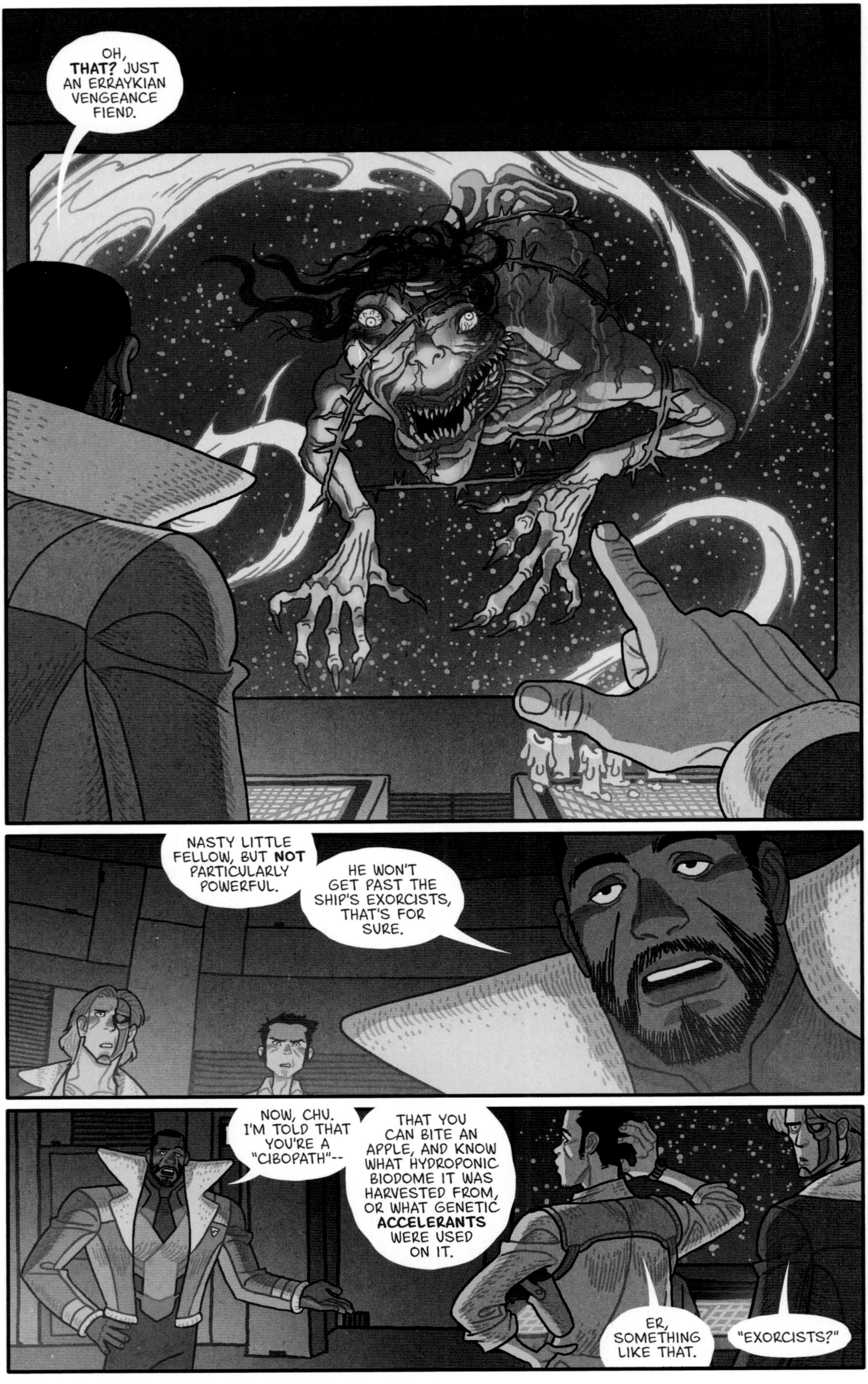
OH, THAT? JUST AN ERRAYKIAN VENGEANCE FIEND.
NASTY LITTLE FELLOW, BUT NOT PARTICULARLY POWERFUL.
HE WON'T GET PAST THE SHIP'S EXORCISTS, THAT'S FOR SURE.
NOW, CHU. I'M TOLD THAT YOU'RE A "CIBOPATH"--
THAT YOU CAN BITE AN APPLE, AND KNOW WHAT HYDROPONIC BIODOME IT WAS HARVESTED FROM, OR WHAT GENETIC ACCELERANTS WERE USED ON IT.
ER, SOMETHING LIKE THAT.
"EXORCISTS?"

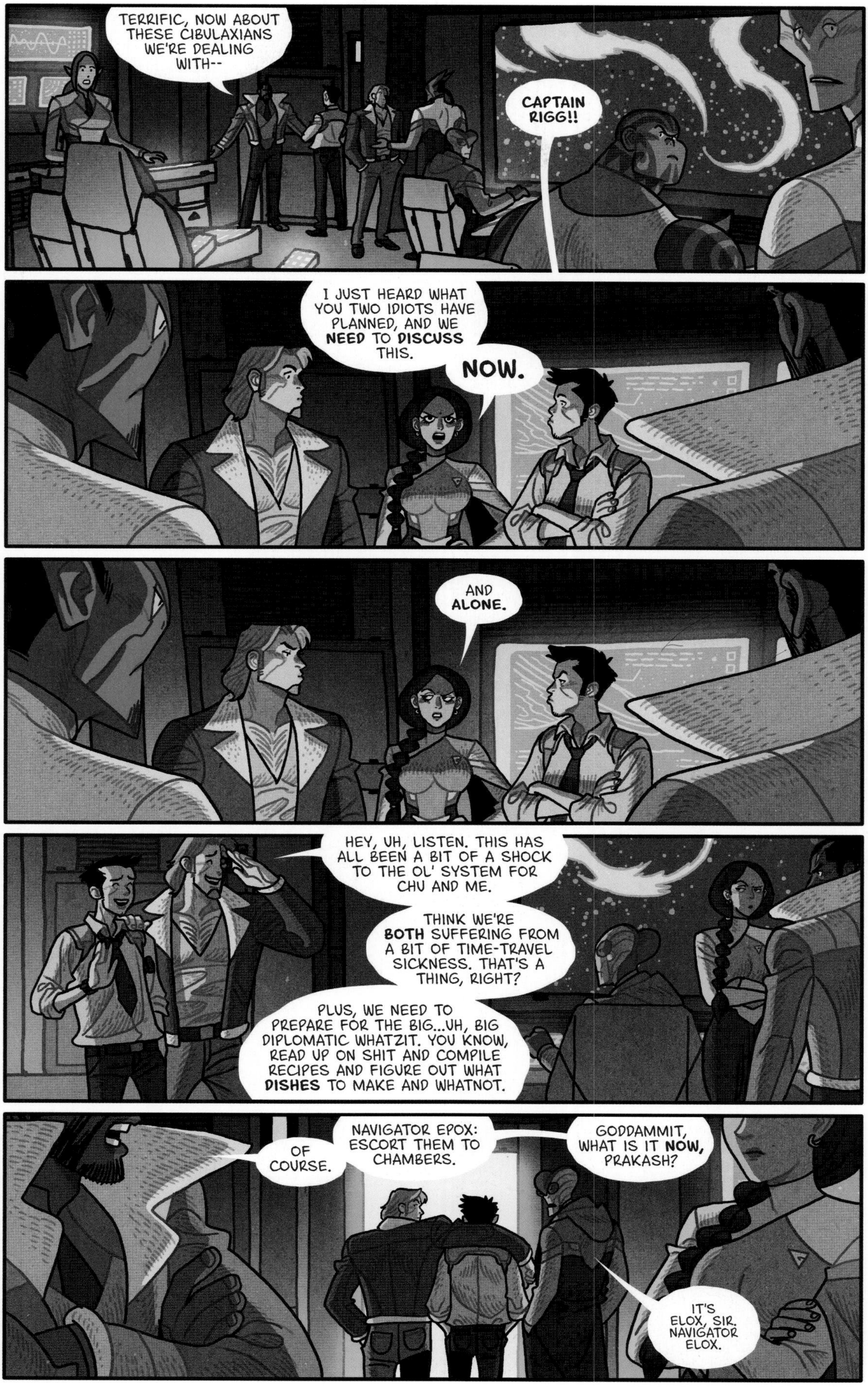
TERRIFIC, NOW ABOUT THESE CIBULAXIANS WE'RE DEALING WITH--
CAPTAIN RIGG!!
I JUST HEARD WHAT YOU TWO IDIOTS HAVE PLANNED, AND WE NEED TO DISCUSS THIS.
NOW.
AND ALONE.
HEY, UH, LISTEN. THIS HAS ALL BEEN A BIT OF A SHOCK TO THE OL' SYSTEM FOR CHU AND ME.
THINK WE'RE BOTH SUFFERING FROM A BIT OF TIME-TRAVEL SICKNESS. THAT'S A THING, RIGHT?
PLUS, WE NEED TO PREPARE FOR THE BIG...UH, BIG DIPLOMATIC WHATZIT. YOU KNOW, READ UP ON SHIT AND COMPILE RECIPES AND FIGURE OUT WHAT DISHES TO MAKE AND WHATNOT.
OF COURSE.
NAVIGATOR EPOX: ESCORT THEM TO CHAMBERS.
GODDAMMIT, WHAT IS IT NOW, PRAKASH?
IT'S ELOX, SIR. NAVIGATOR ELOX.

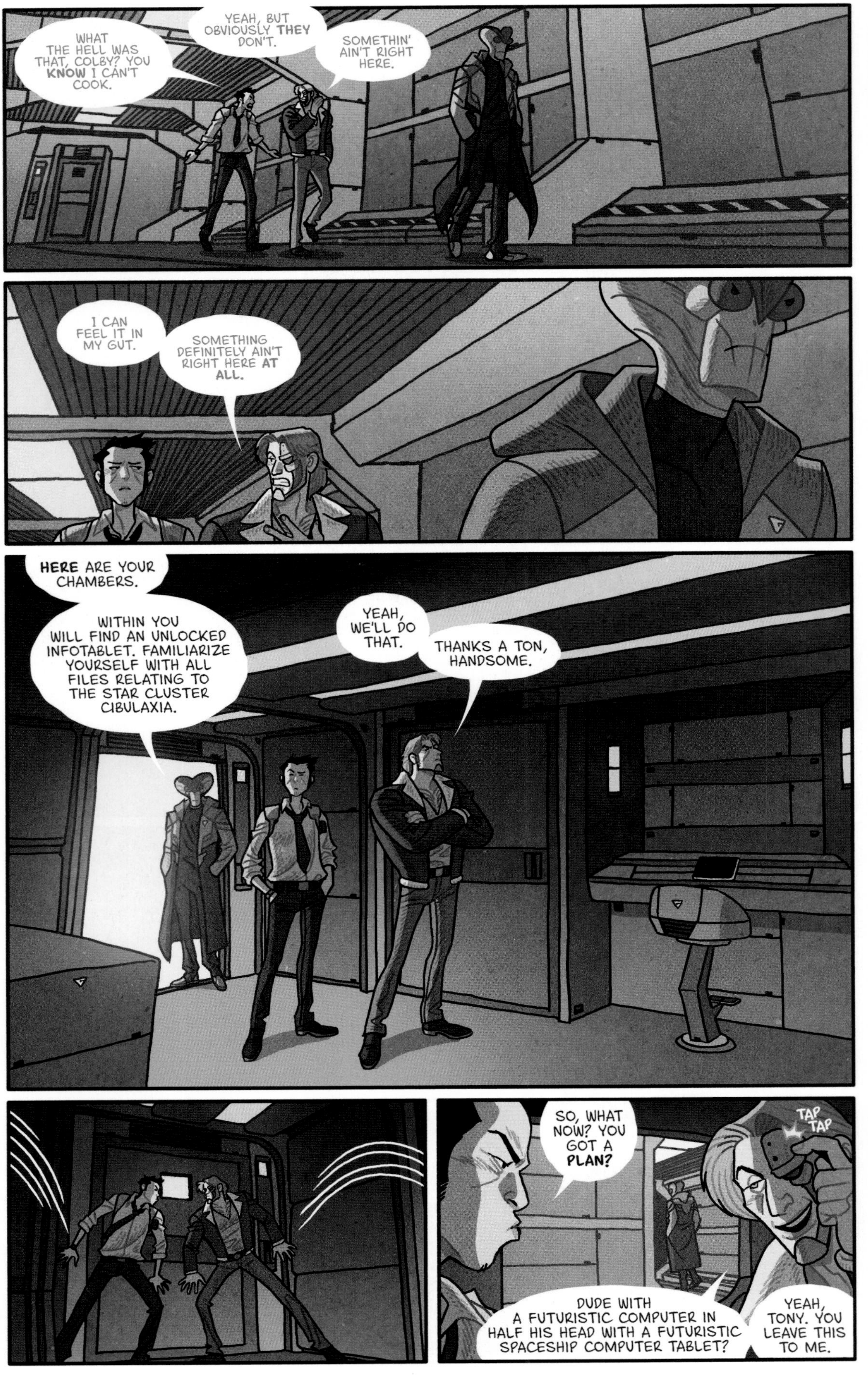
WHAT THE HELL WAS THAT, COLBY? YOU KNOW I CAN'T COOK.
YEAH, BUT OBVIOUSLY THEY DON'T.
SOMETHIN' AIN'T RIGHT HERE.
I CAN FEEL IT IN MY GUT.
SOMETHING DEFINITELY AIN'T RIGHT HERE AT ALL.
HERE ARE YOUR CHAMBERS.
WITHIN YOU WILL FIND AN UNLOCKED INFOTABLET. FAMILIARIZE YOURSELF WITH ALL FILES RELATING TO THE STAR CLUSTER CIBULAXIA.
YEAH, WE'LL DO THAT.
THANKS A TON, HANDSOME.
SO, WHAT NOW? YOU GOT A PLAN?
TAP TAP
DUDE WITH A FUTURISTIC COMPUTER IN HALF HIS HEAD WITH A FUTURISTIC SPACESHIP COMPUTER TABLET?
YEAH, TONY. YOU LEAVE THIS TO ME.

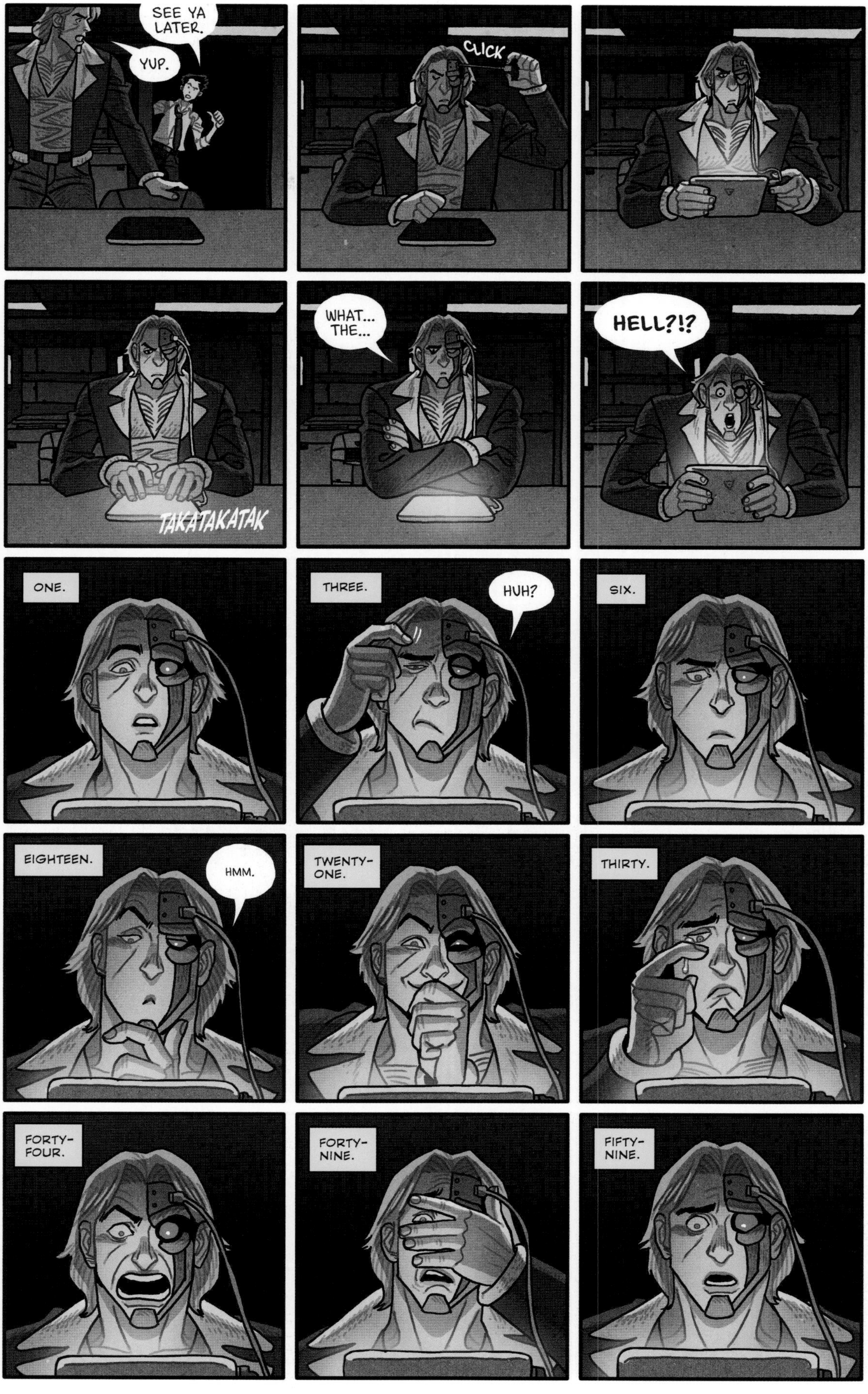

SEE YA LATER.
YUP.
CLICK
TAKATAKATAK
WHAT... THE...
HELL?!?
ONE.
THREE.
HUH?
SIX.
EIGHTEEN.
HMM.
TWENTY-ONE.
THIRTY.
FORTY-FOUR.
FORTY-NINE.
FIFTY-NINE.

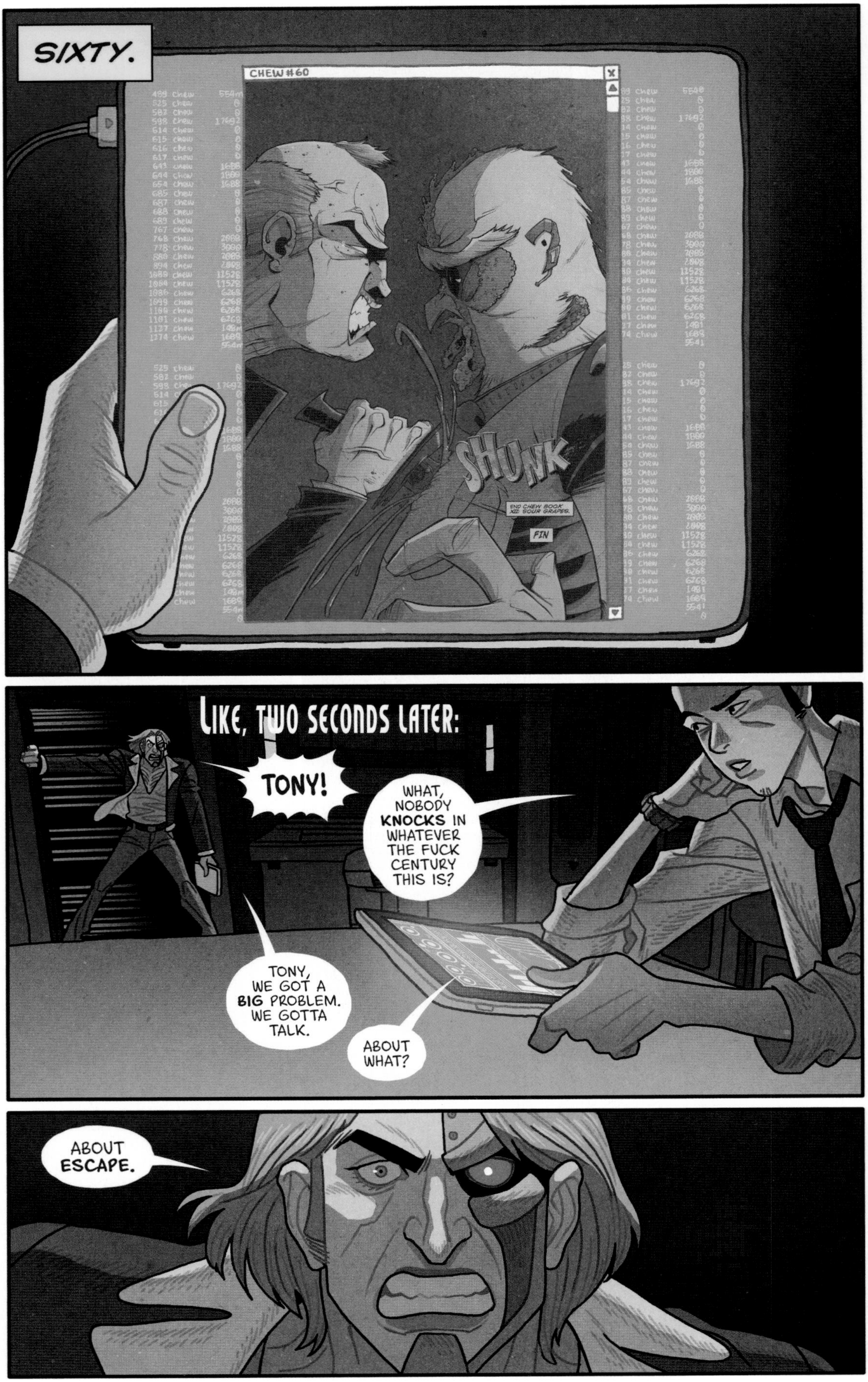
SIXTY.
CHEW #60
SHUNK
END CHEW BOOK XII: SOUR GRAPES.
FIN
LIKE, TWO SECONDS LATER:
TONY!
WHAT, NOBODY KNOCKS IN WHATEVER THE FUCK CENTURY THIS IS?
TONY, WE GOT A BIG PROBLEM. WE GOTTA TALK.
ABOUT WHAT?
ABOUT ESCAPE.

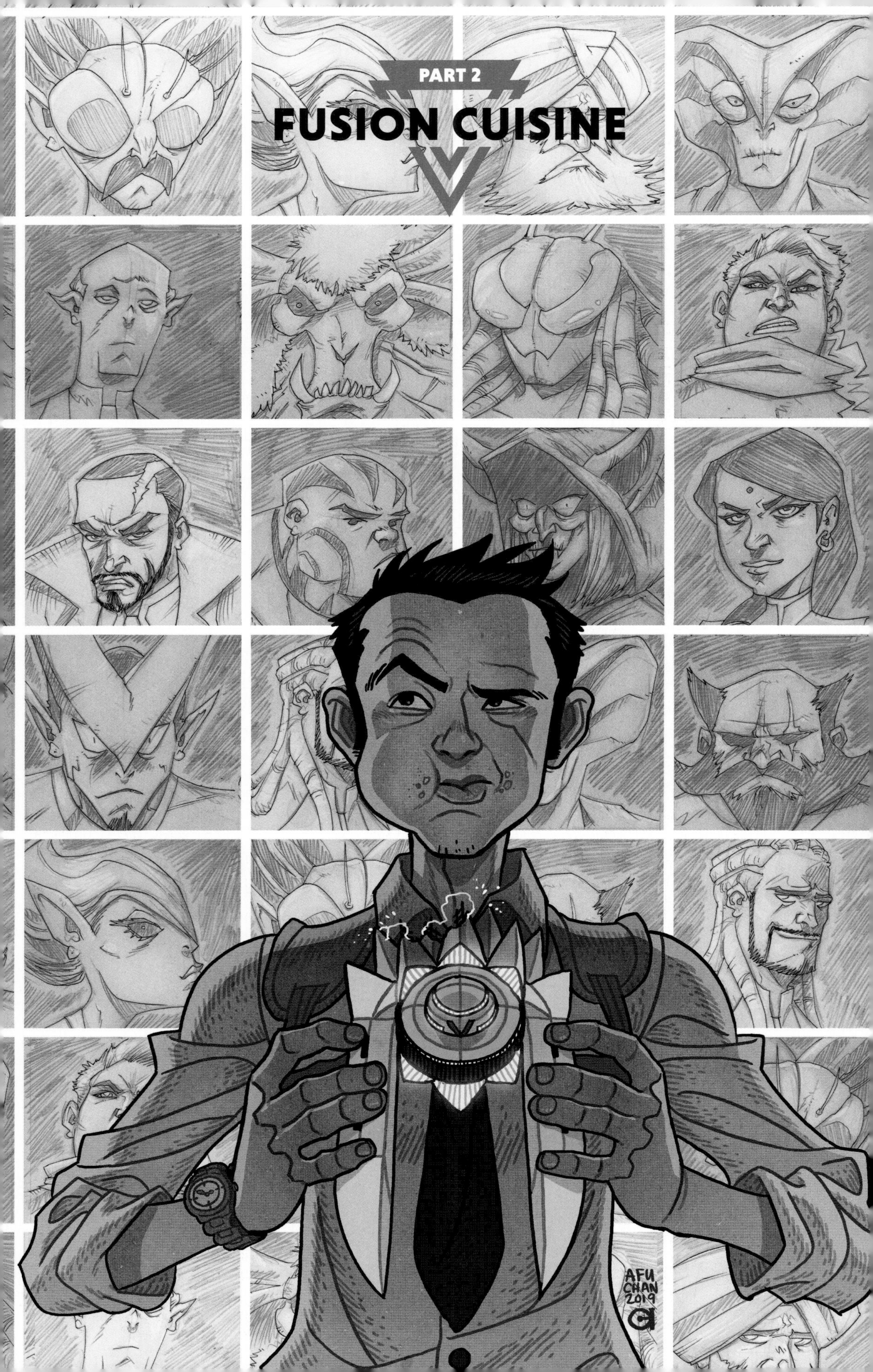
PART 2
FUSION CUISINE
AFU CHAN 2019

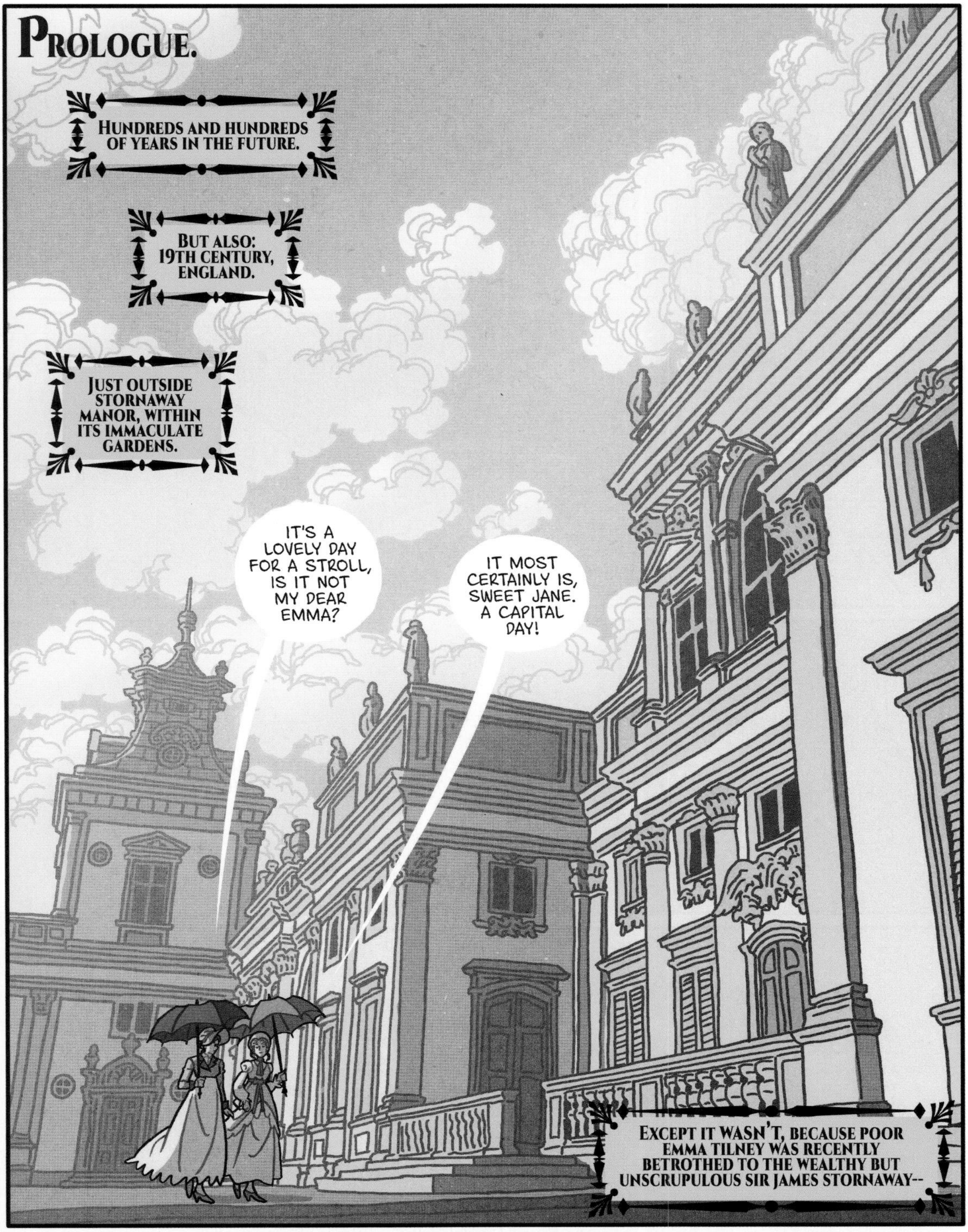
PROLOGUE.
HUNDREDS AND HUNDREDS OF YEARS IN THE FUTURE.
BUT ALSO: 19TH CENTURY, ENGLAND.
JUST OUTSIDE STORNAWAY MANOR, WITHIN ITS IMMACULATE GARDENS.
IT'S A LOVELY DAY FOR A STROLL, IS IT NOT MY DEAR EMMA?
IT MOST CERTAINLY IS, SWEET JANE. A CAPITAL DAY!
EXCEPT IT WASN'T, BECAUSE POOR EMMA TILNEY WAS RECENTLY BETROTHED TO THE WEALTHY BUT UNSCRUPULOUS SIR JAMES STORNAWAY--

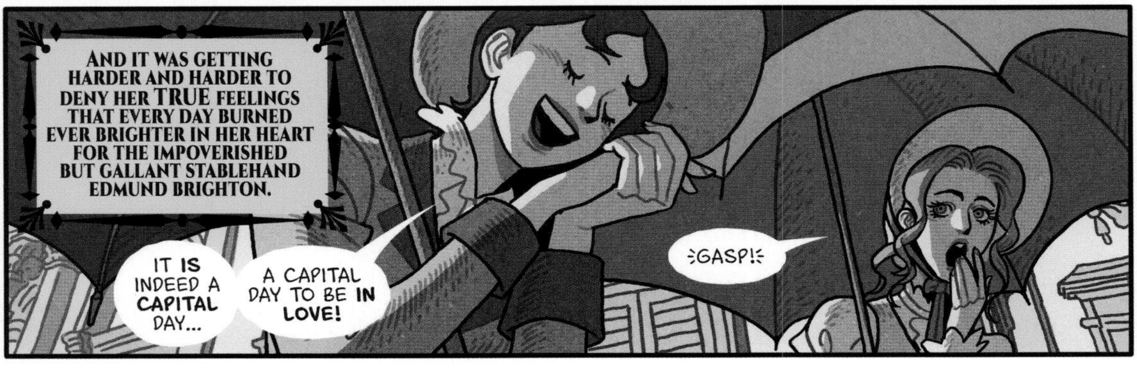
AND IT WAS GETTING HARDER AND HARDER TO DENY HER TRUE FEELINGS THAT EVERY DAY BURNED EVER BRIGHTER IN HER HEART FOR THE IMPOVERISHED BUT GALLANT STABLEHAND EDMUND BRIGHTON.
IT IS INDEED A CAPITAL DAY...
A CAPITAL DAY TO BE IN LOVE!
GASP!

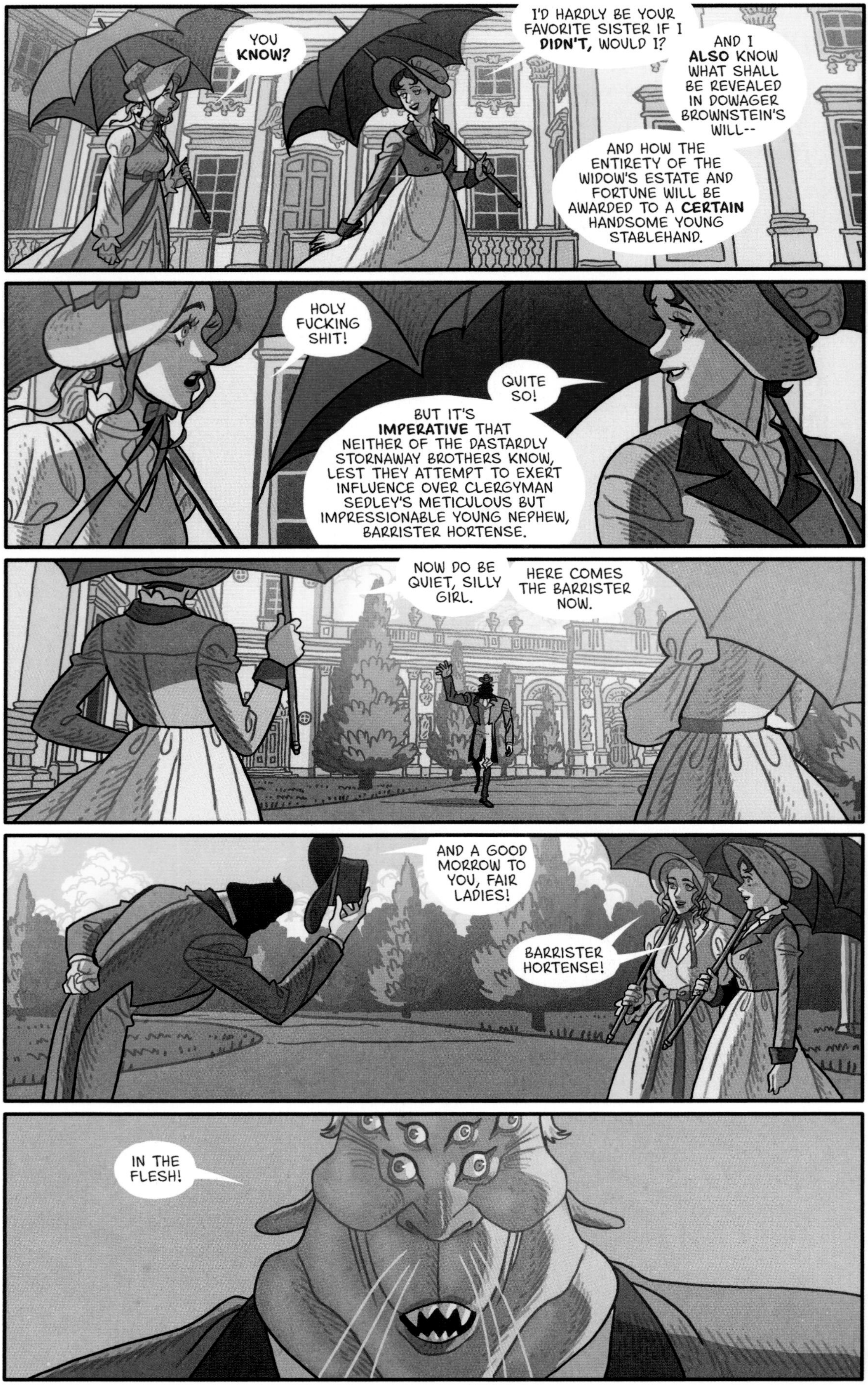
YOU **KNOW?**
I'D HARDLY BE YOUR FAVORITE SISTER IF I **DIDN'T,** WOULD I?
AND I **ALSO** KNOW WHAT SHALL BE REVEALED IN DOWAGER BROWNSTEIN'S WILL--
AND HOW THE ENTIRETY OF THE WIDOW'S ESTATE AND FORTUNE WILL BE AWARDED TO A **CERTAIN** HANDSOME YOUNG STABLEHAND.
HOLY FUCKING SHIT!
QUITE SO!
BUT IT'S **IMPERATIVE** THAT NEITHER OF THE DASTARDLY STORNAWAY BROTHERS KNOW, LEST THEY ATTEMPT TO EXERT INFLUENCE OVER CLERGYMAN SEDLEY'S METICULOUS BUT IMPRESSIONABLE YOUNG NEPHEW, BARRISTER HORTENSE.
NOW DO BE QUIET, SILLY GIRL.
HERE COMES THE BARRISTER NOW.
AND A GOOD MORROW TO YOU, FAIR LADIES!
BARRISTER HORTENSE!
IN THE FLESH!

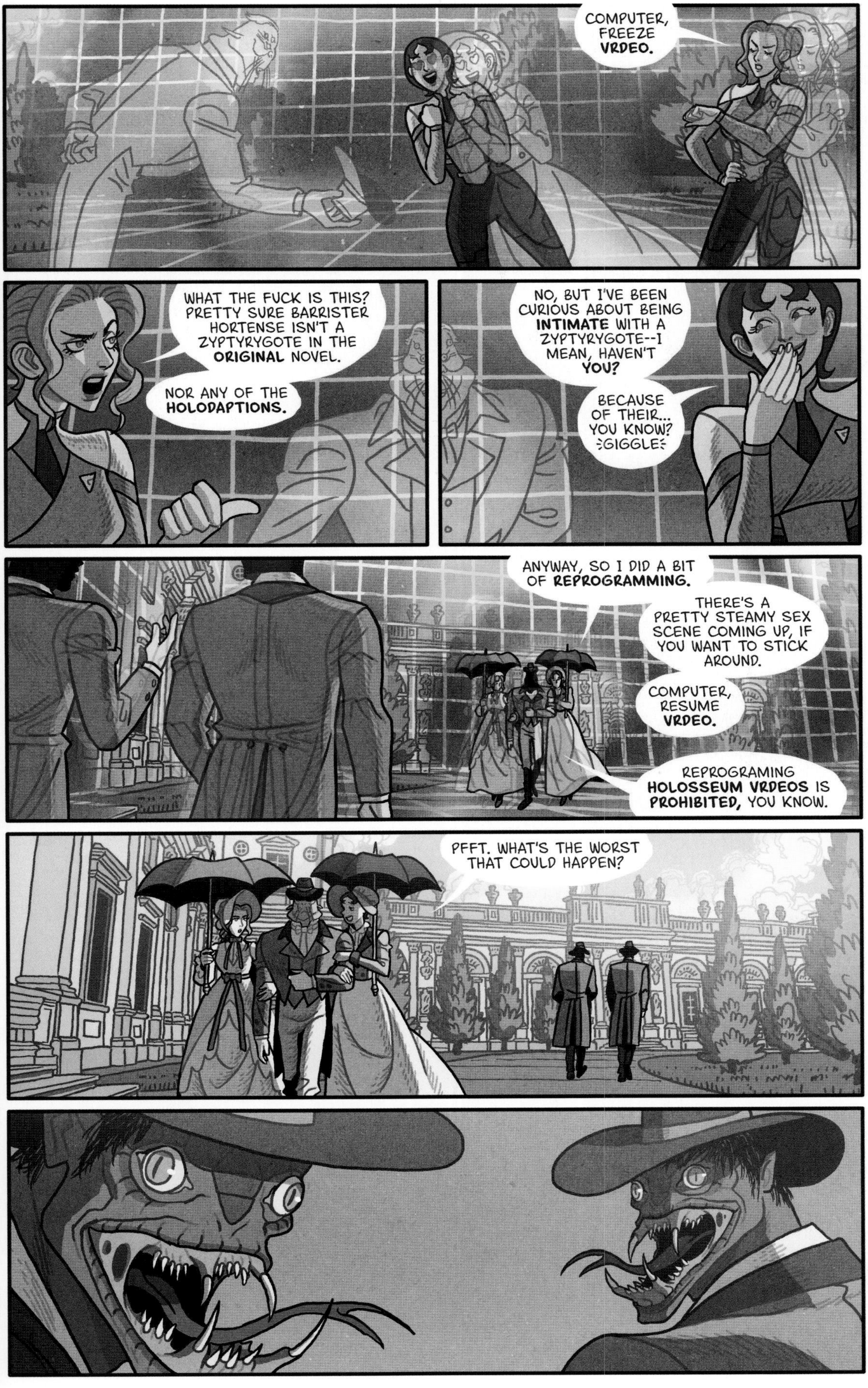
COMPUTER, FREEZE VRDEO.
WHAT THE FUCK IS THIS? PRETTY SURE BARRISTER HORTENSE ISN'T A ZYPTYRYGOTE IN THE ORIGINAL NOVEL.
NOR ANY OF THE HOLODAPTIONS.
NO, BUT I'VE BEEN CURIOUS ABOUT BEING INTIMATE WITH A ZYPTYRYGOTE--I MEAN, HAVEN'T YOU?
BECAUSE OF THEIR... YOU KNOW? GIGGLE
ANYWAY, SO I DID A BIT OF REPROGRAMMING.
THERE'S A PRETTY STEAMY SEX SCENE COMING UP, IF YOU WANT TO STICK AROUND.
COMPUTER, RESUME VRDEO.
REPROGRAMING HOLOSSEUM VRDEOS IS PROHIBITED, YOU KNOW.
PFFT. WHAT'S THE WORST THAT COULD HAPPEN?

"THIS.

"**THIS** IS THE WORST THAT CAN HAPPEN.

"WE CREATE AN ARTIFICIAL DIGITAL REALITY, AND SOMETHING **INFERNAL** FINDS ITS WAY INTO THE SYSTEM.

"THEN ALL **HELL** BREAKS LOOSE. USUALLY **LITERALLY**."

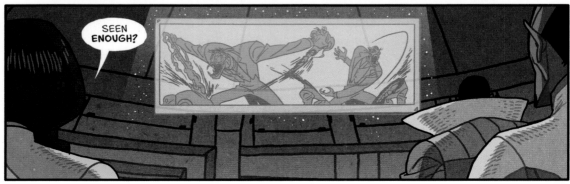

SEEN **ENOUGH?**

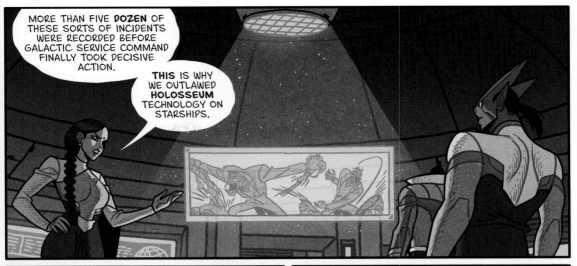

MORE THAN FIVE **DOZEN** OF THESE SORTS OF INCIDENTS WERE RECORDED BEFORE GALACTIC SERVICE COMMAND FINALLY TOOK DECISIVE ACTION.

THIS IS WHY WE OUTLAWED **HOLOSSEUM** TECHNOLOGY ON STARSHIPS.

THIS IS NOT **JUST** AGAINST REGULATIONS, BUT IT'S **HIGHLY** AGAINST REGULATIONS.

I KNOW BUCKING GALACTIC SERVICE PROTOCOL IS KINDA CAPTAIN RIGG'S **THING**, WEARISOME AS IT IS...

BUT, HONESTLY, FIRST OFFICER SATALIS, I EXPECTED BETTER OF **YOU.**

YOU MADE IT **QUITE** CLEAR HOW IMPORTANT THE **ADMIRAL** THOUGHT A TRADE ROUTE AGREEMENT WITH THE CIBULAXIANS WAS.

I THOUGHT A **FOOD-PSYCHIC DETECTIVE** HELPING US WITH **FOOD-COMMUNICATING ALIENS** WAS A **GOOD** IDEA.

RISKING EVERYONE ABOARD **THE CHARON** IS A BAD IDEA.

THEY'RE JUST **COMIC BOOK** CHARACTERS. HARMLESS CARTOONS WE BROUGHT TO HOLOGRAPHIC LIFE FROM SOME OLD CHILDREN'S STORY.

THEY **THINK** WE BROUGHT THEM HERE VIA **TIME TRAVEL.**

THEN YOU BETTER HOPE THEY **DON'T** FIND OUT THE **TRUTH.**

AS YOU SAID, YOU BROUGHT THEM TO **LIFE.**

THEY **WON'T** TAKE TOO KINDLY TO BEING CONSIGNED BACK TO **OBLIVION** JUST AS SOON AS **YOU'RE** THROUGH WITH THEM.

END PROLOGUE.

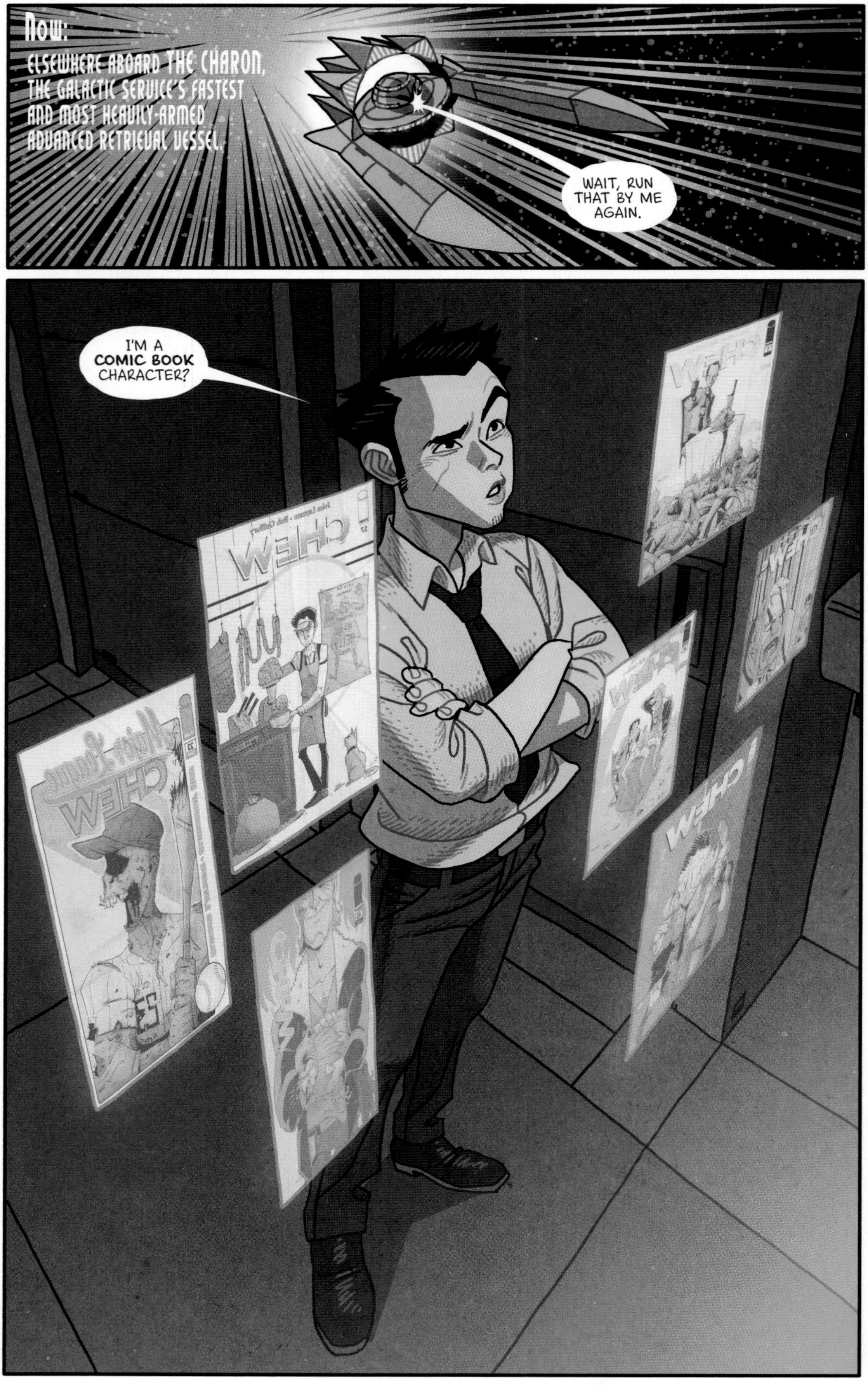
Now:
Elsewhere aboard The Charon, the Galactic Service's fastest and most heavily-armed advanced retrieval vessel.
WAIT, RUN THAT BY ME AGAIN.
I'M A COMIC BOOK CHARACTER?

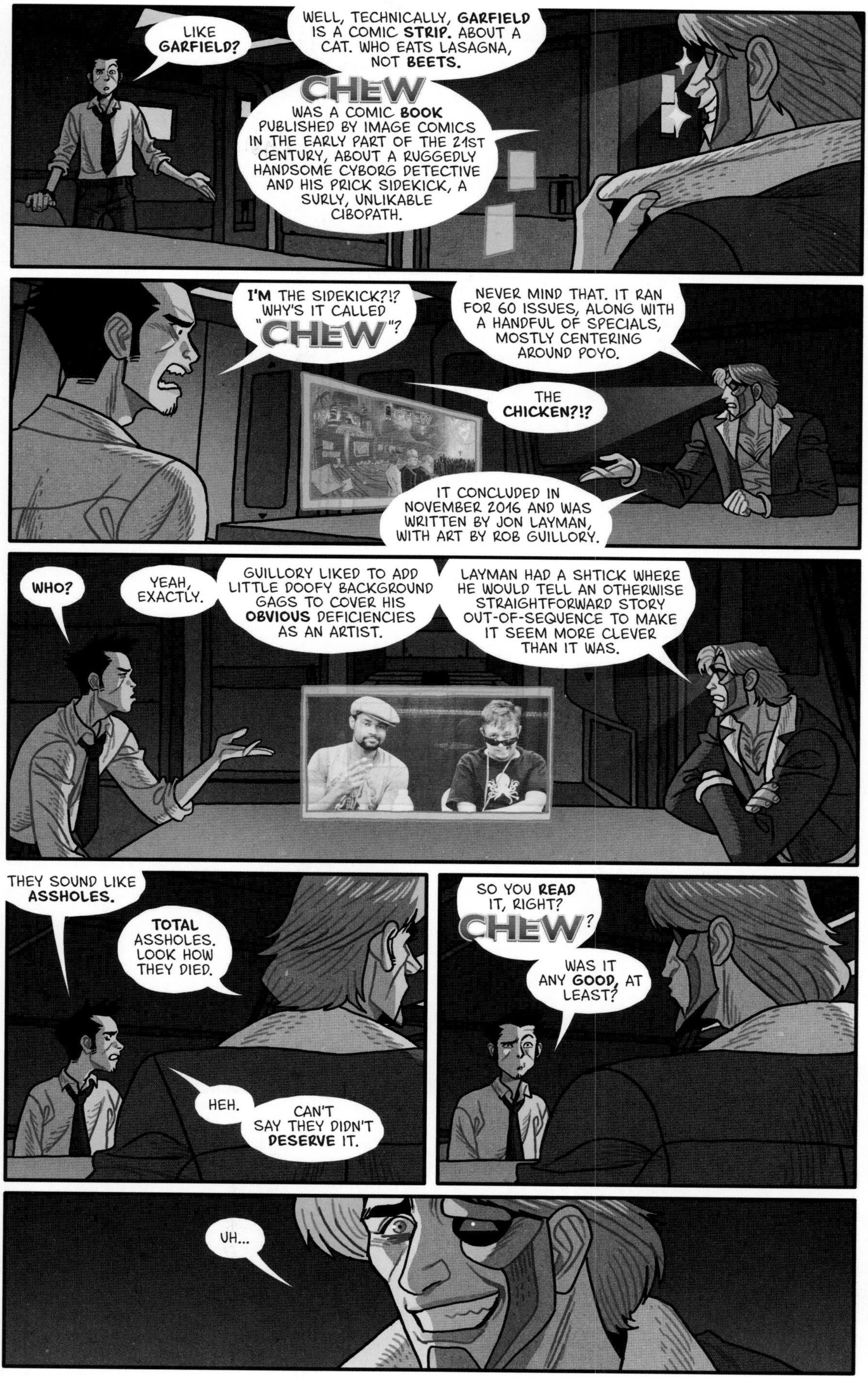
LIKE GARFIELD?
WELL, TECHNICALLY, GARFIELD IS A COMIC STRIP. ABOUT A CAT. WHO EATS LASAGNA, NOT BEETS.
CHEW WAS A COMIC BOOK PUBLISHED BY IMAGE COMICS IN THE EARLY PART OF THE 21ST CENTURY, ABOUT A RUGGEDLY HANDSOME CYBORG DETECTIVE AND HIS PRICK SIDEKICK, A SURLY, UNLIKABLE CIBOPATH.
I'M THE SIDEKICK?!? WHY'S IT CALLED "CHEW"?
NEVER MIND THAT. IT RAN FOR 60 ISSUES, ALONG WITH A HANDFUL OF SPECIALS, MOSTLY CENTERING AROUND POYO.
THE CHICKEN?!?
IT CONCLUDED IN NOVEMBER 2016 AND WAS WRITTEN BY JON LAYMAN, WITH ART BY ROB GUILLORY.
WHO?
YEAH, EXACTLY.
GUILLORY LIKED TO ADD LITTLE DOOFY BACKGROUND GAGS TO COVER HIS OBVIOUS DEFICIENCIES AS AN ARTIST.
LAYMAN HAD A SHTICK WHERE HE WOULD TELL AN OTHERWISE STRAIGHTFORWARD STORY OUT-OF-SEQUENCE TO MAKE IT SEEM MORE CLEVER THAN IT WAS.
THEY SOUND LIKE ASSHOLES.
TOTAL ASSHOLES. LOOK HOW THEY DIED.
HEH.
CAN'T SAY THEY DIDN'T DESERVE IT.
SO YOU READ IT, RIGHT? CHEW?
WAS IT ANY GOOD, AT LEAST?
UH...

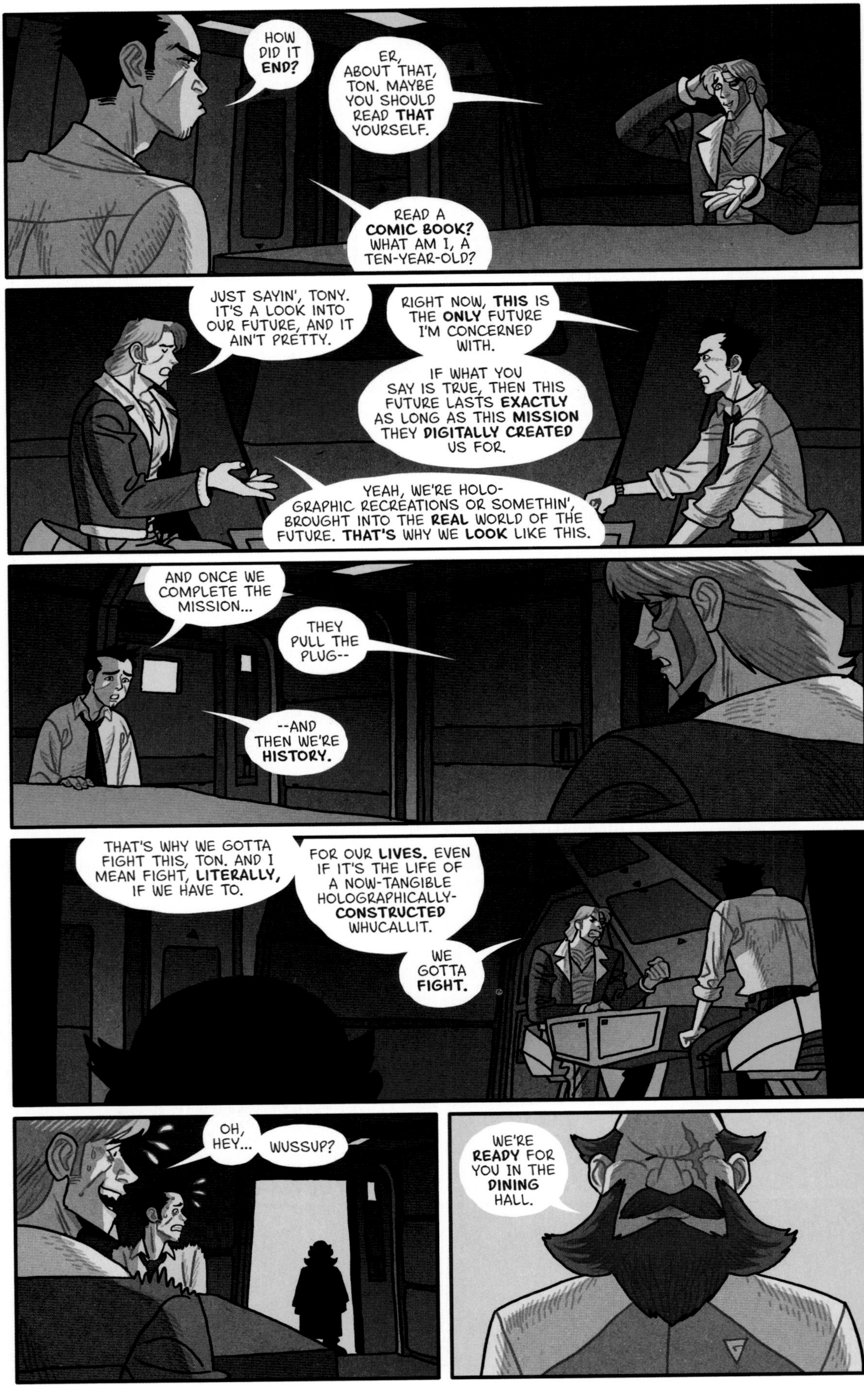
HOW DID IT END?
ER, ABOUT THAT, TON. MAYBE YOU SHOULD READ THAT YOURSELF.
READ A COMIC BOOK? WHAT AM I, A TEN-YEAR-OLD?
JUST SAYIN', TONY. IT'S A LOOK INTO OUR FUTURE, AND IT AIN'T PRETTY.
RIGHT NOW, THIS IS THE ONLY FUTURE I'M CONCERNED WITH.
IF WHAT YOU SAY IS TRUE, THEN THIS FUTURE LASTS EXACTLY AS LONG AS THIS MISSION THEY DIGITALLY CREATED US FOR.
YEAH, WE'RE HOLO-GRAPHIC RECREATIONS OR SOMETHIN', BROUGHT INTO THE REAL WORLD OF THE FUTURE. THAT'S WHY WE LOOK LIKE THIS.
AND ONCE WE COMPLETE THE MISSION...
THEY PULL THE PLUG--
--AND THEN WE'RE HISTORY.
THAT'S WHY WE GOTTA FIGHT THIS, TON. AND I MEAN FIGHT, LITERALLY, IF WE HAVE TO.
FOR OUR LIVES. EVEN IF IT'S THE LIFE OF A NOW-TANGIBLE HOLOGRAPHICALLY-CONSTRUCTED WHUCALLIT.
WE GOTTA FIGHT.
OH, HEY...
WUSSUP?
WE'RE READY FOR YOU IN THE DINING HALL.

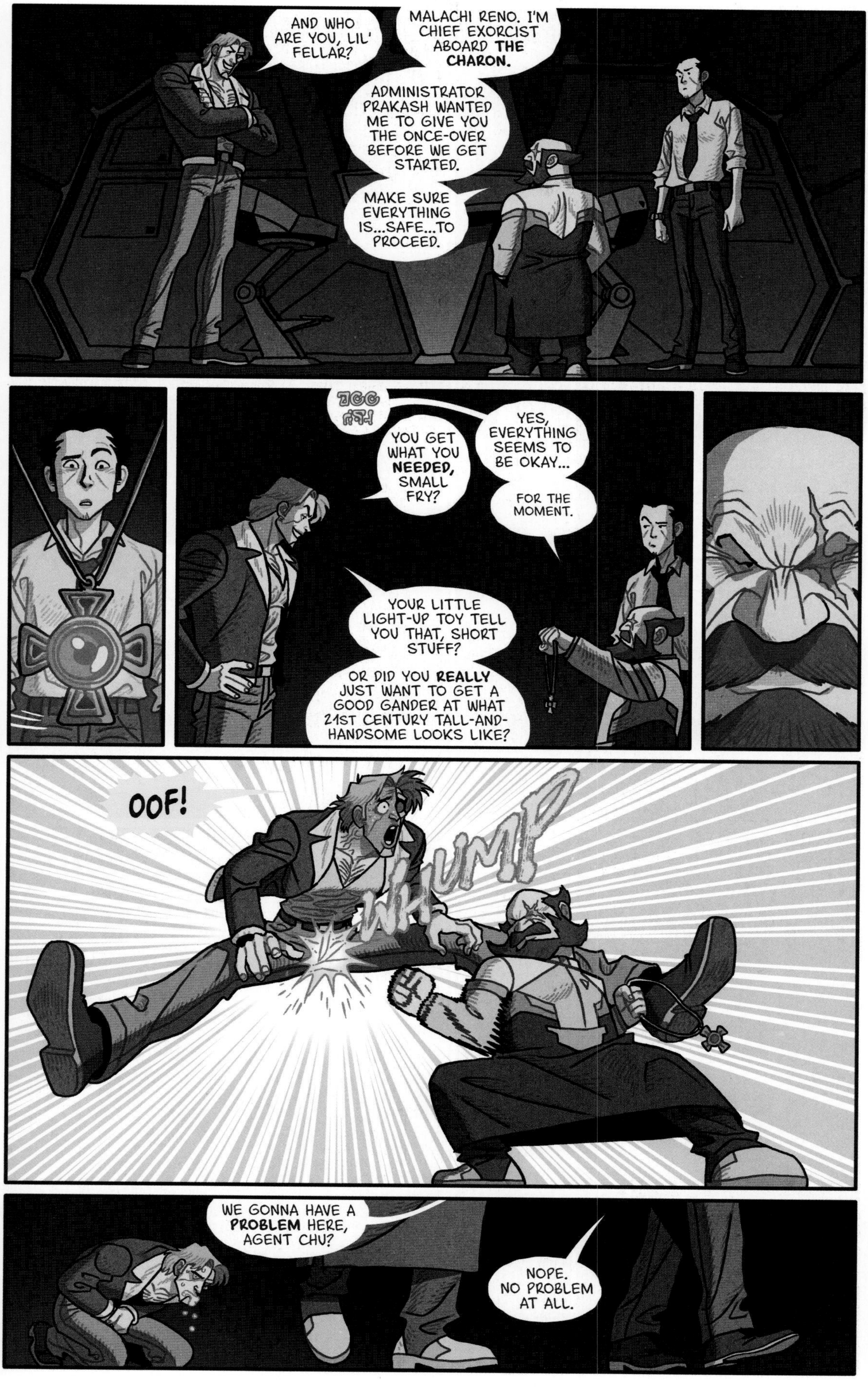
AND WHO ARE YOU, LIL' FELLAR?
MALACHI RENO. I'M CHIEF EXORCIST ABOARD **THE CHARON.**
ADMINISTRATOR PRAKASH WANTED ME TO GIVE YOU THE ONCE-OVER BEFORE WE GET STARTED.
MAKE SURE EVERYTHING IS...SAFE...TO PROCEED.
YOU GET WHAT YOU **NEEDED,** SMALL FRY?
YES, EVERYTHING SEEMS TO BE OKAY...
FOR THE MOMENT.
YOUR LITTLE LIGHT-UP TOY TELL YOU THAT, SHORT STUFF?
OR DID YOU **REALLY** JUST WANT TO GET A GOOD GANDER AT WHAT 21ST CENTURY TALL-AND-HANDSOME LOOKS LIKE?
OOF!
WHUMP
WE GONNA HAVE A **PROBLEM** HERE, AGENT CHU?
NOPE. NO PROBLEM AT ALL.

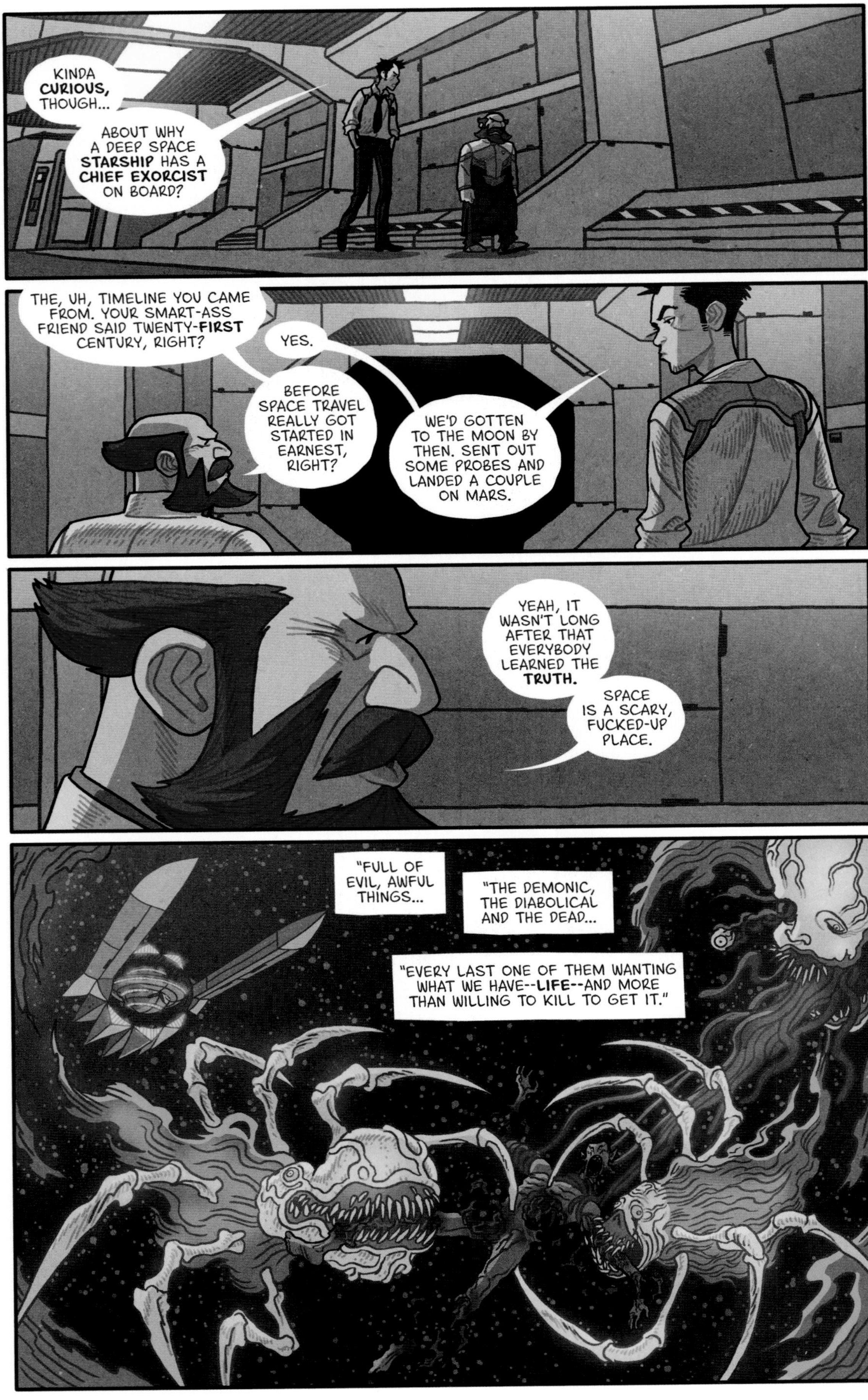
KINDA CURIOUS, THOUGH...
ABOUT WHY A DEEP SPACE STARSHIP HAS A CHIEF EXORCIST ON BOARD?
THE, UH, TIMELINE YOU CAME FROM. YOUR SMART-ASS FRIEND SAID TWENTY-FIRST CENTURY, RIGHT?
YES.
BEFORE SPACE TRAVEL REALLY GOT STARTED IN EARNEST, RIGHT?
WE'D GOTTEN TO THE MOON BY THEN. SENT OUT SOME PROBES AND LANDED A COUPLE ON MARS.
YEAH, IT WASN'T LONG AFTER THAT EVERYBODY LEARNED THE TRUTH.
SPACE IS A SCARY, FUCKED-UP PLACE.
"FULL OF EVIL, AWFUL THINGS...
"THE DEMONIC, THE DIABOLICAL AND THE DEAD...
"EVERY LAST ONE OF THEM WANTING WHAT WE HAVE--LIFE--AND MORE THAN WILLING TO KILL TO GET IT."

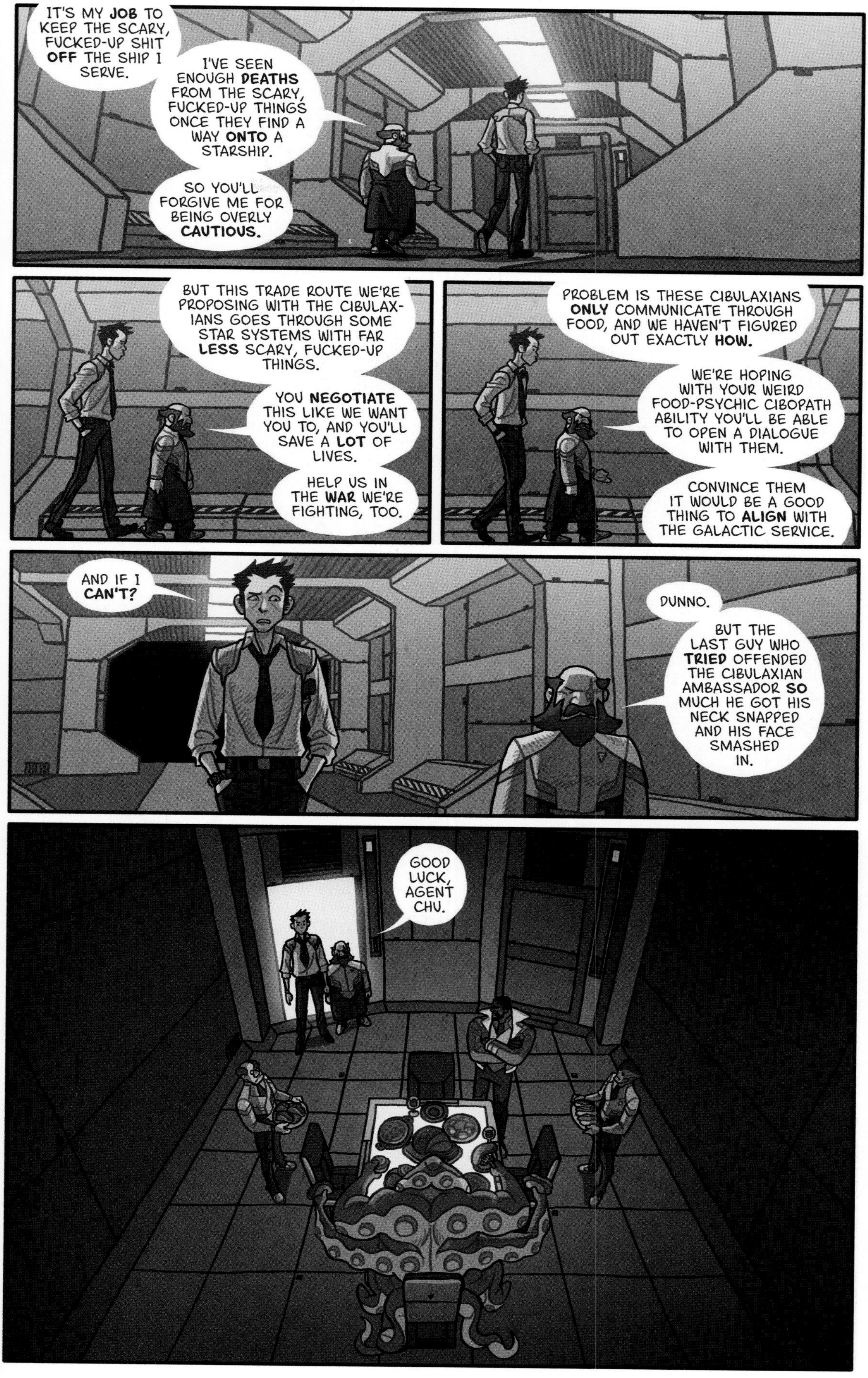
IT'S MY JOB TO KEEP THE SCARY, FUCKED-UP SHIT OFF THE SHIP I SERVE.
I'VE SEEN ENOUGH DEATHS FROM THE SCARY, FUCKED-UP THINGS ONCE THEY FIND A WAY ONTO A STARSHIP.
SO YOU'LL FORGIVE ME FOR BEING OVERLY CAUTIOUS.
BUT THIS TRADE ROUTE WE'RE PROPOSING WITH THE CIBULAX-IANS GOES THROUGH SOME STAR SYSTEMS WITH FAR LESS SCARY, FUCKED-UP THINGS.
YOU NEGOTIATE THIS LIKE WE WANT YOU TO, AND YOU'LL SAVE A LOT OF LIVES.
HELP US IN THE WAR WE'RE FIGHTING, TOO.
PROBLEM IS THESE CIBULAXIANS ONLY COMMUNICATE THROUGH FOOD, AND WE HAVEN'T FIGURED OUT EXACTLY HOW.
WE'RE HOPING WITH YOUR WEIRD FOOD-PSYCHIC CIBOPATH ABILITY YOU'LL BE ABLE TO OPEN A DIALOGUE WITH THEM.
CONVINCE THEM IT WOULD BE A GOOD THING TO ALIGN WITH THE GALACTIC SERVICE.
AND IF I CAN'T?
DUNNO.
BUT THE LAST GUY WHO TRIED OFFENDED THE CIBULAXIAN AMBASSADOR SO MUCH HE GOT HIS NECK SNAPPED AND HIS FACE SMASHED IN.
GOOD LUCK, AGENT CHU.

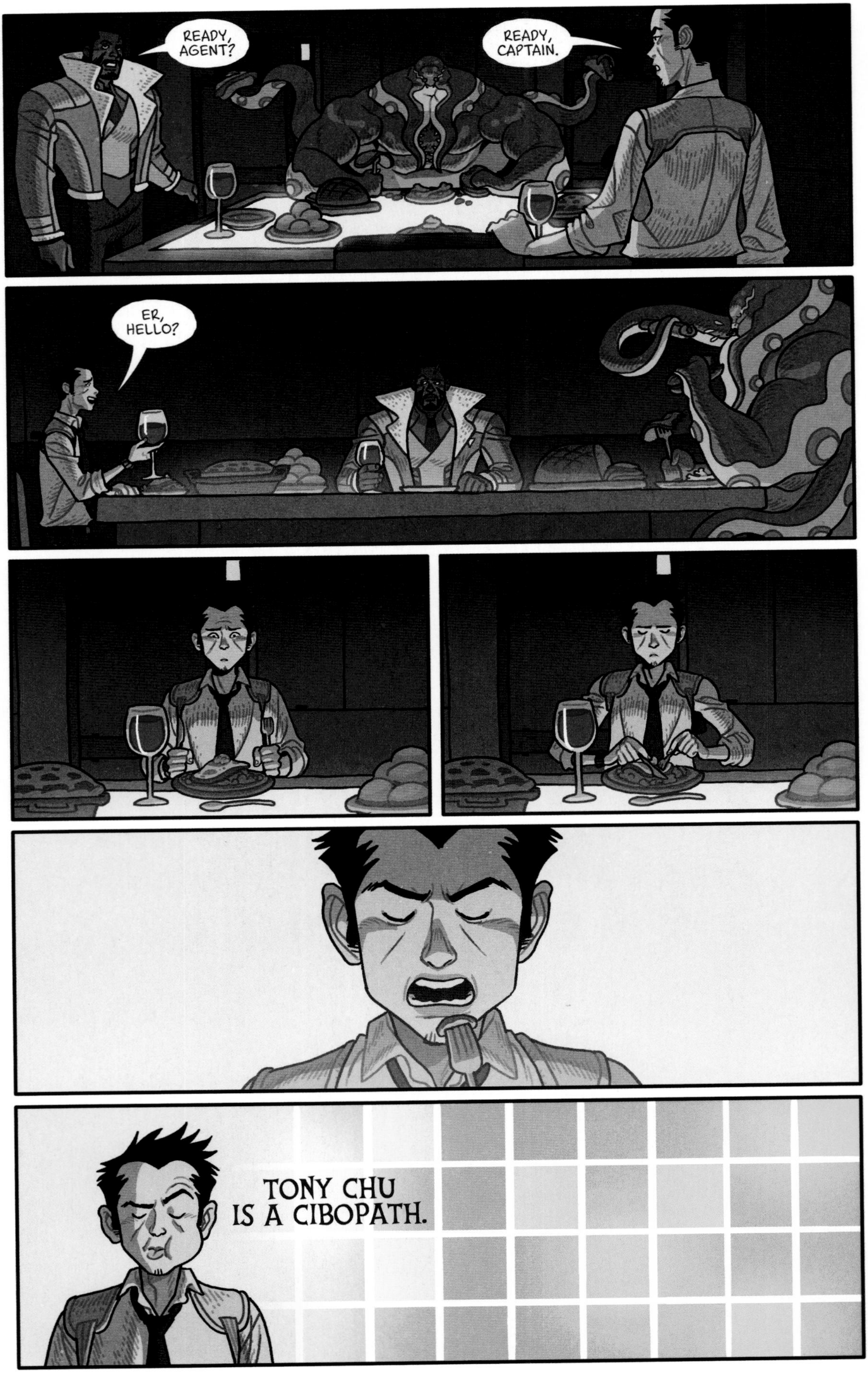
READY, AGENT?
READY, CAPTAIN.
ER, HELLO?
TONY CHU IS A CIBOPATH.

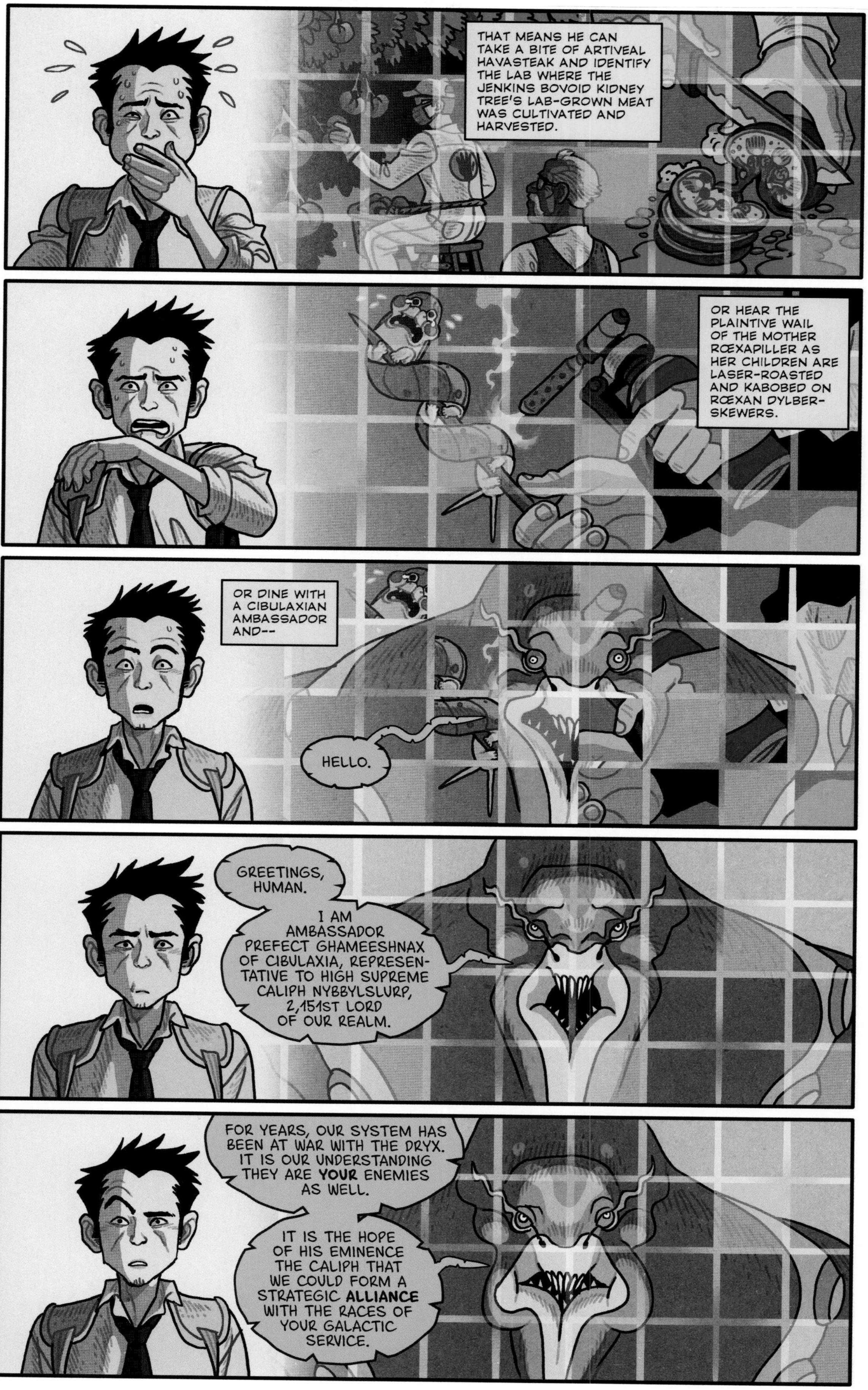
THAT MEANS HE CAN TAKE A BITE OF ARTIVEAL HAVASTEAK AND IDENTIFY THE LAB WHERE THE JENKINS BOVOID KIDNEY TREE'S LAB-GROWN MEAT WAS CULTIVATED AND HARVESTED.
OR HEAR THE PLAINTIVE WAIL OF THE MOTHER RŒXAPILLER AS HER CHILDREN ARE LASER-ROASTED AND KABOBED ON RŒXAN DYLBER-SKEWERS.
OR DINE WITH A CIBULAXIAN AMBASSADOR AND--
HELLO.
GREETINGS, HUMAN.
I AM AMBASSADOR PREFECT GHAMEESHNAX OF CIBULAXIA, REPRESENTATIVE TO HIGH SUPREME CALIPH NYBBYLSLURP, 2,151ST LORD OF OUR REALM.
FOR YEARS, OUR SYSTEM HAS BEEN AT WAR WITH THE DRYX. IT IS OUR UNDERSTANDING THEY ARE **YOUR** ENEMIES AS WELL.
IT IS THE HOPE OF HIS EMINENCE THE CALIPH THAT WE COULD FORM A STRATEGIC **ALLIANCE** WITH THE RACES OF YOUR GALACTIC SERVICE.

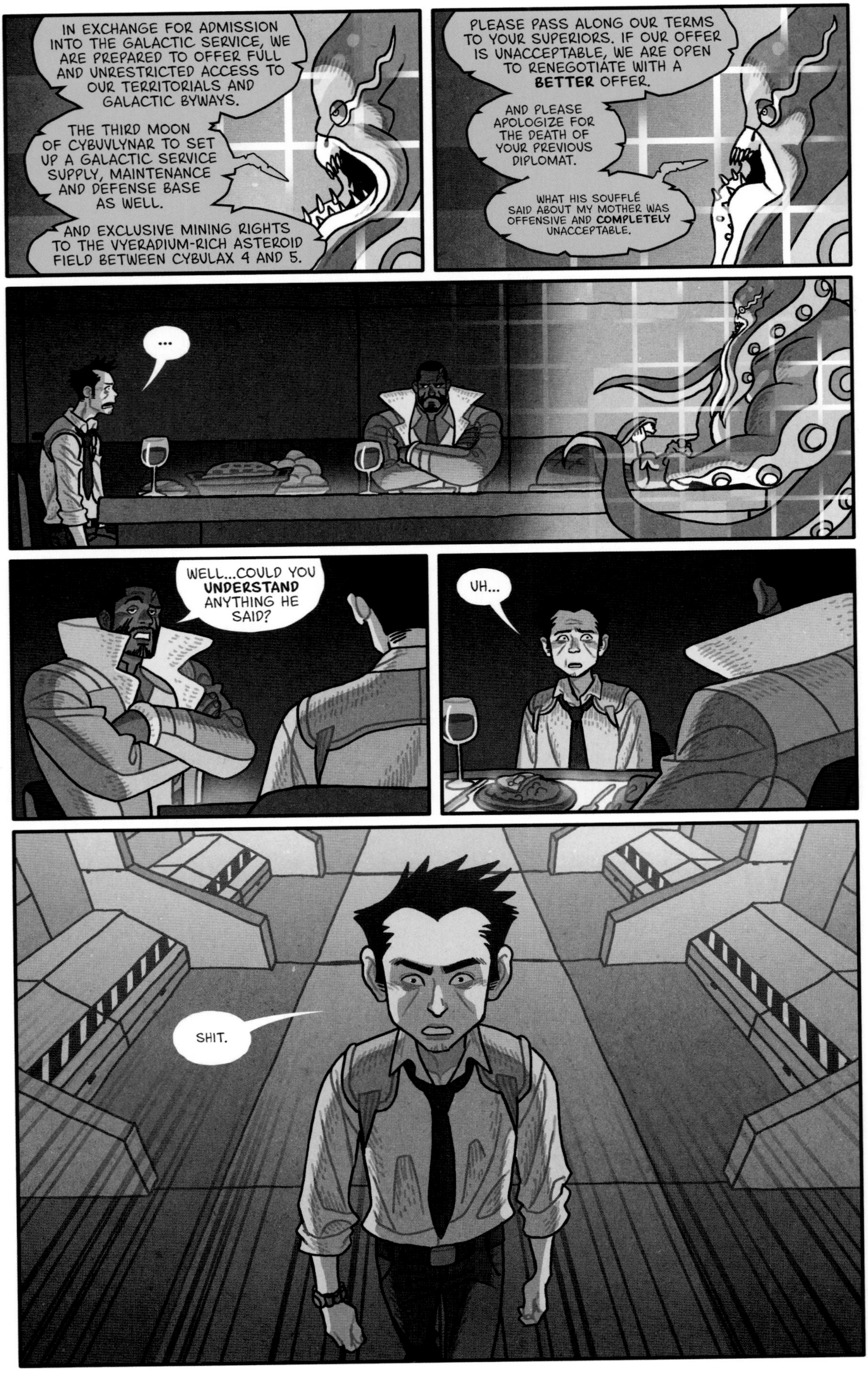
IN EXCHANGE FOR ADMISSION INTO THE GALACTIC SERVICE, WE ARE PREPARED TO OFFER FULL AND UNRESTRICTED ACCESS TO OUR TERRITORIALS AND GALACTIC BYWAYS.
THE THIRD MOON OF CYBUVLYNAR TO SET UP A GALACTIC SERVICE SUPPLY, MAINTENANCE AND DEFENSE BASE AS WELL.
AND EXCLUSIVE MINING RIGHTS TO THE VYERADIUM-RICH ASTEROID FIELD BETWEEN CYBULAX 4 AND 5.
PLEASE PASS ALONG OUR TERMS TO YOUR SUPERIORS. IF OUR OFFER IS UNACCEPTABLE, WE ARE OPEN TO RENEGOTIATE WITH A **BETTER** OFFER.
AND PLEASE APOLOGIZE FOR THE DEATH OF YOUR PREVIOUS DIPLOMAT.
WHAT HIS SOUFFLÉ SAID ABOUT MY MOTHER WAS OFFENSIVE AND **COMPLETELY** UNACCEPTABLE.
...
WELL...COULD YOU **UNDERSTAND** ANYTHING HE SAID?
UH...
SHIT.

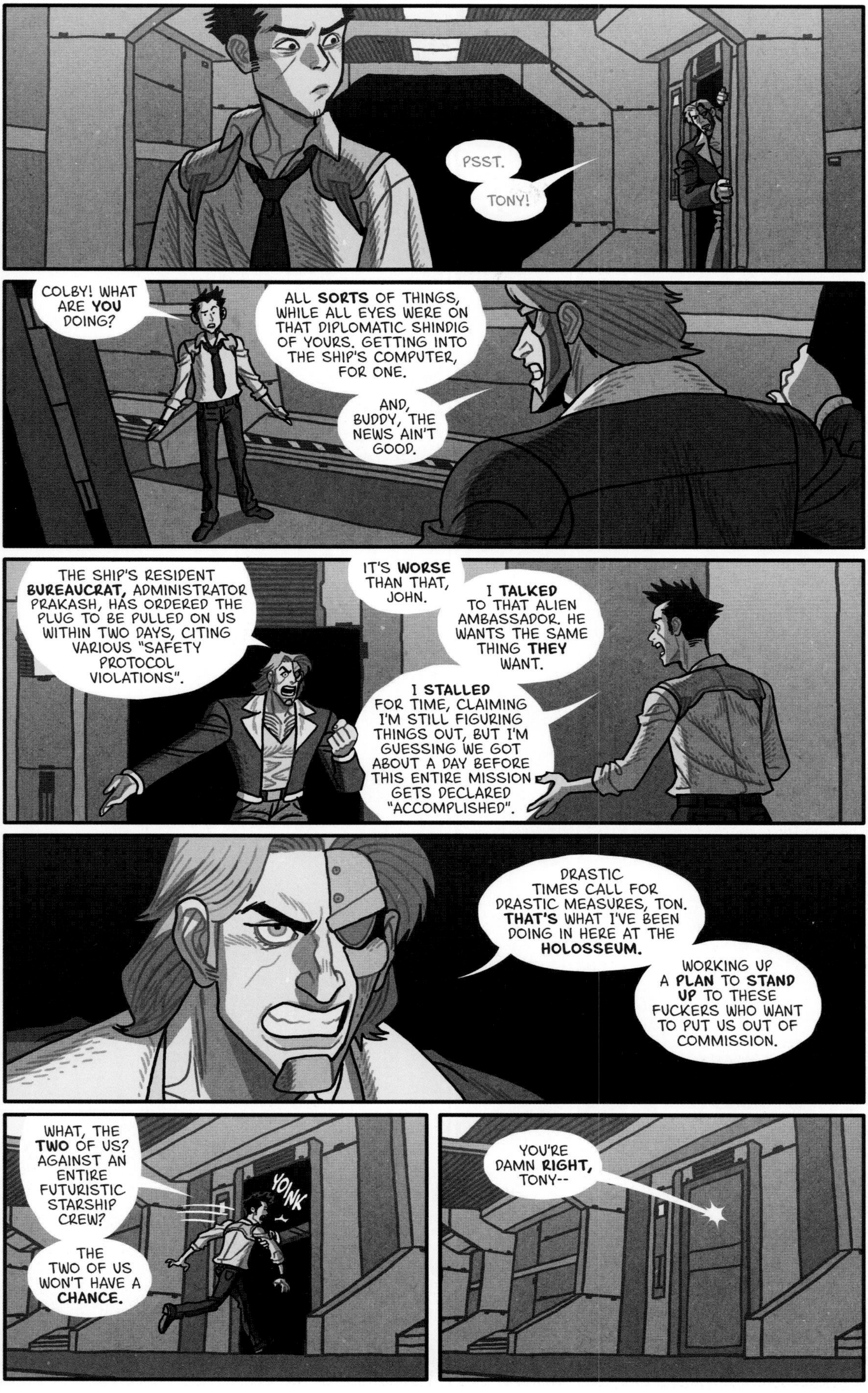
PSST.
TONY!
COLBY! WHAT ARE YOU DOING?
ALL SORTS OF THINGS, WHILE ALL EYES WERE ON THAT DIPLOMATIC SHINDIG OF YOURS. GETTING INTO THE SHIP'S COMPUTER, FOR ONE.
AND, BUDDY, THE NEWS AIN'T GOOD.
THE SHIP'S RESIDENT BUREAUCRAT, ADMINISTRATOR PRAKASH, HAS ORDERED THE PLUG TO BE PULLED ON US WITHIN TWO DAYS, CITING VARIOUS "SAFETY PROTOCOL VIOLATIONS".
IT'S WORSE THAN THAT, JOHN.
I TALKED TO THAT ALIEN AMBASSADOR. HE WANTS THE SAME THING THEY WANT.
I STALLED FOR TIME, CLAIMING I'M STILL FIGURING THINGS OUT, BUT I'M GUESSING WE GOT ABOUT A DAY BEFORE THIS ENTIRE MISSION GETS DECLARED "ACCOMPLISHED".
DRASTIC TIMES CALL FOR DRASTIC MEASURES, TON. THAT'S WHAT I'VE BEEN DOING IN HERE AT THE HOLOSSEUM.
WORKING UP A PLAN TO STAND UP TO THESE FUCKERS WHO WANT TO PUT US OUT OF COMMISSION.
WHAT, THE TWO OF US? AGAINST AN ENTIRE FUTURISTIC STARSHIP CREW?
THE TWO OF US WON'T HAVE A CHANCE.
YOINK
YOU'RE DAMN RIGHT, TONY--

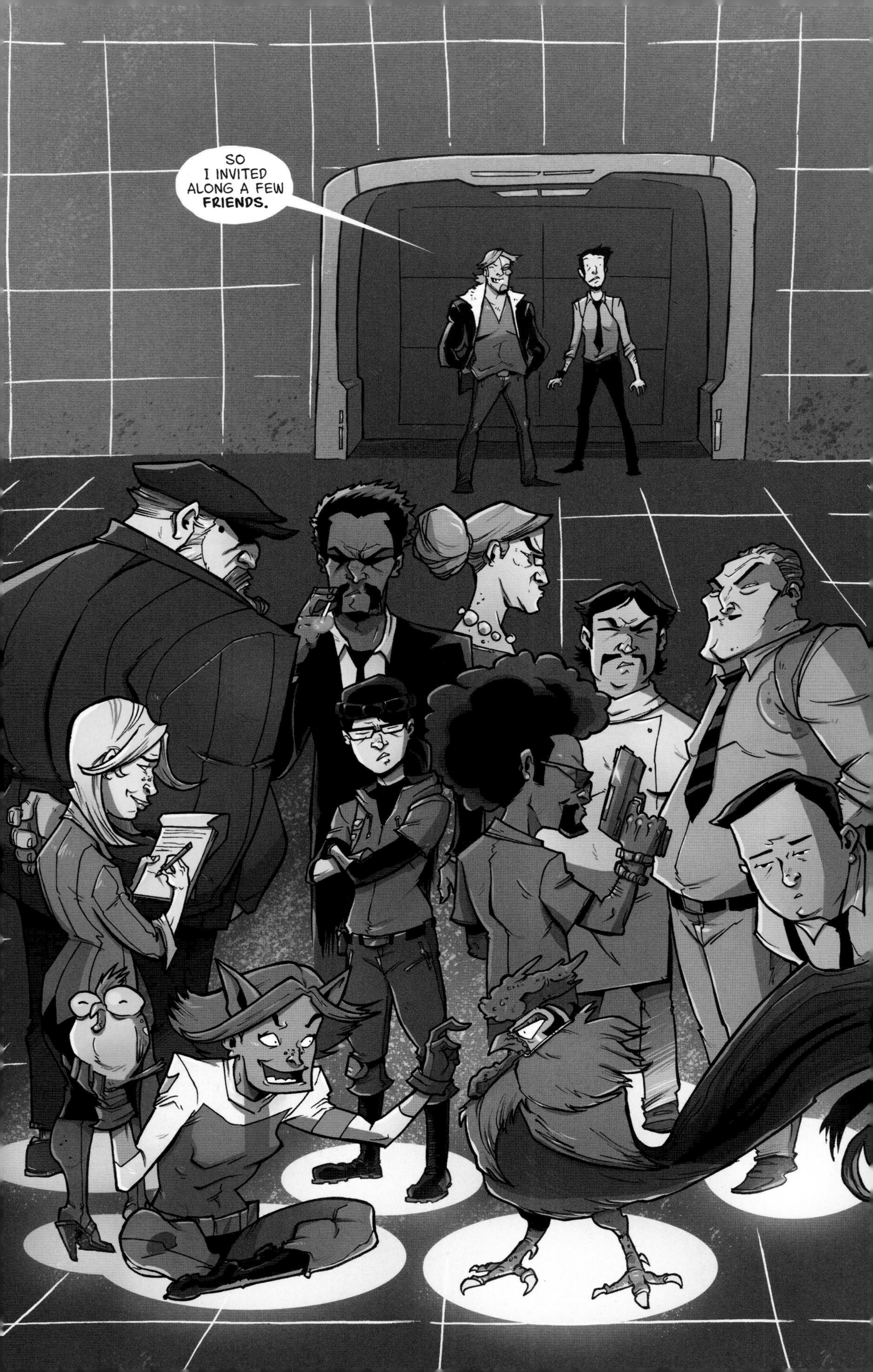
SO I INVITED ALONG A FEW FRIENDS.

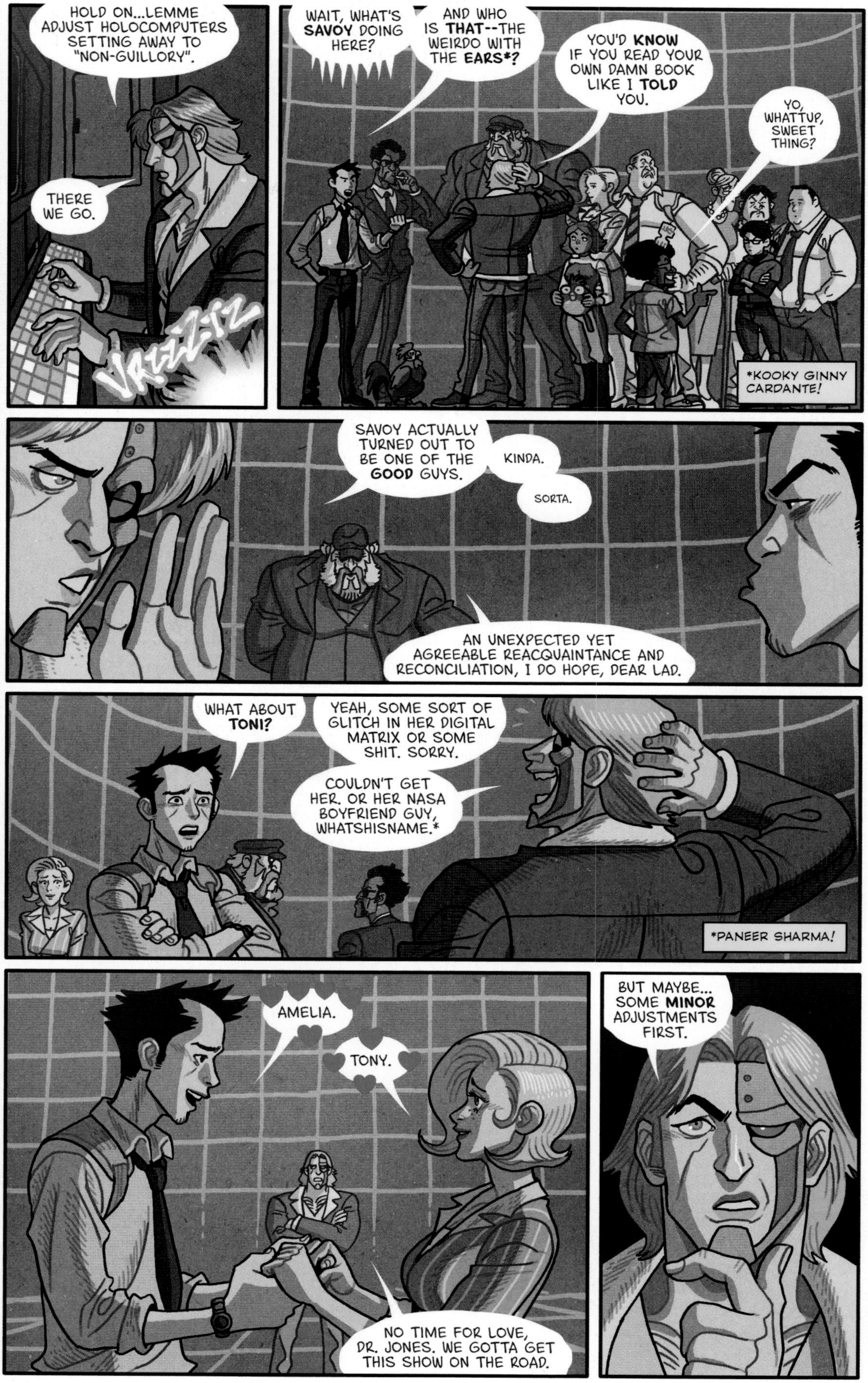
HOLD ON...LEMME ADJUST HOLOCOMPUTERS SETTING AWAY TO "NON-GUILLORY".
THERE WE GO.
VRZZZZZ
WAIT, WHAT'S **SAVOY** DOING HERE?
AND WHO IS **THAT**--THE WEIRDO WITH THE **EARS***?
YOU'D **KNOW** IF YOU READ YOUR OWN DAMN BOOK LIKE I **TOLD** YOU.
YO, WHATTUP, SWEET THING?
*KOOKY GINNY CARDANTE!
SAVOY ACTUALLY TURNED OUT TO BE ONE OF THE **GOOD** GUYS.
KINDA.
SORTA.
AN UNEXPECTED YET AGREEABLE REACQUAINTANCE AND RECONCILIATION, I DO HOPE, DEAR LAD.
WHAT ABOUT **TONI?**
YEAH, SOME SORT OF GLITCH IN HER DIGITAL MATRIX OR SOME SHIT. SORRY.
COULDN'T GET HER. OR HER NASA BOYFRIEND GUY, WHATSHISNAME.*
*PANEER SHARMA!
AMELIA.
TONY.
NO TIME FOR LOVE, DR. JONES. WE GOTTA GET THIS SHOW ON THE ROAD.
BUT MAYBE... SOME **MINOR** ADJUSTMENTS FIRST.

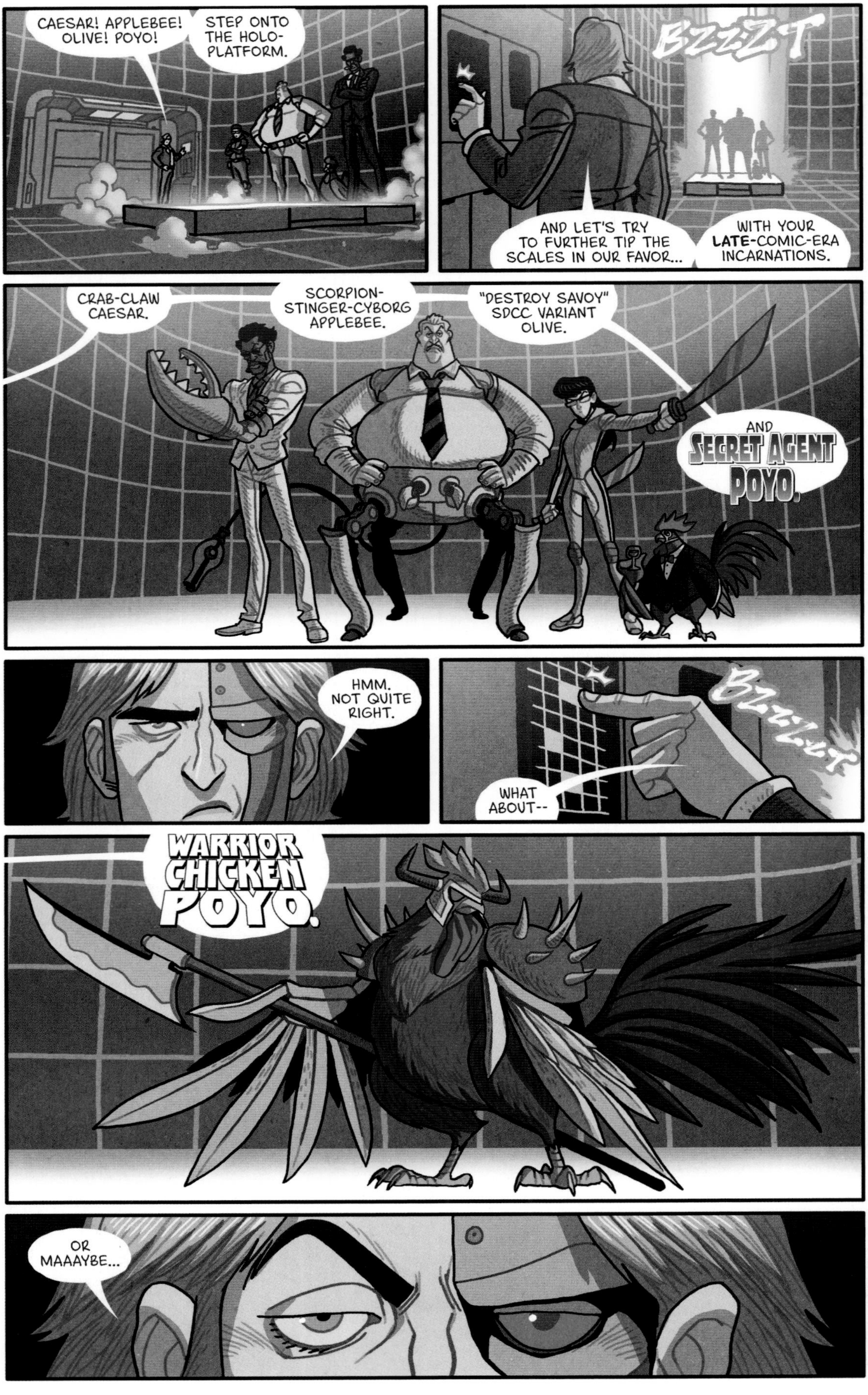
CAESAR! APPLEBEE! OLIVE! POYO!
STEP ONTO THE HOLO-PLATFORM.
BZZZT
AND LET'S TRY TO FURTHER TIP THE SCALES IN OUR FAVOR...
WITH YOUR **LATE**-COMIC-ERA INCARNATIONS.
CRAB-CLAW CAESAR.
SCORPION-STINGER-CYBORG APPLEBEE.
"DESTROY SAVOY" SDCC VARIANT OLIVE.
AND SECRET AGENT POYO.
HMM. NOT QUITE RIGHT.
BZZZZT
WHAT ABOUT--
WARRIOR CHICKEN POYO.
OR MAAAYBE...

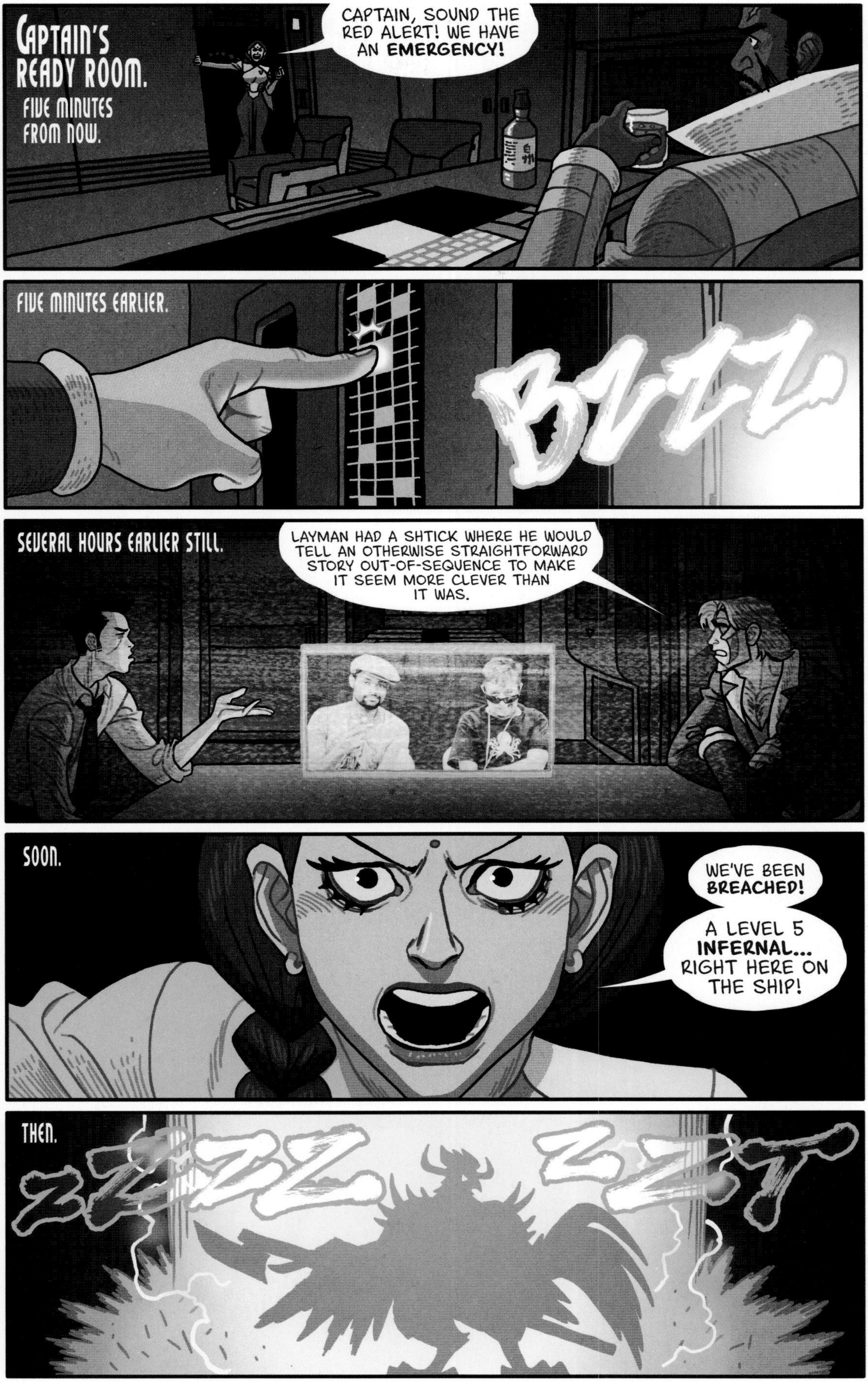
CAPTAIN'S READY ROOM.
FIVE MINUTES FROM NOW.
CAPTAIN, SOUND THE RED ALERT! WE HAVE AN EMERGENCY!
FIVE MINUTES EARLIER.
BZZZ
SEVERAL HOURS EARLIER STILL.
LAYMAN HAD A SHTICK WHERE HE WOULD TELL AN OTHERWISE STRAIGHTFORWARD STORY OUT-OF-SEQUENCE TO MAKE IT SEEM MORE CLEVER THAN IT WAS.
SOON.
WE'VE BEEN BREACHED!
A LEVEL 5 INFERNAL... RIGHT HERE ON THE SHIP!
THEN.
ZZZZZ ZZZT

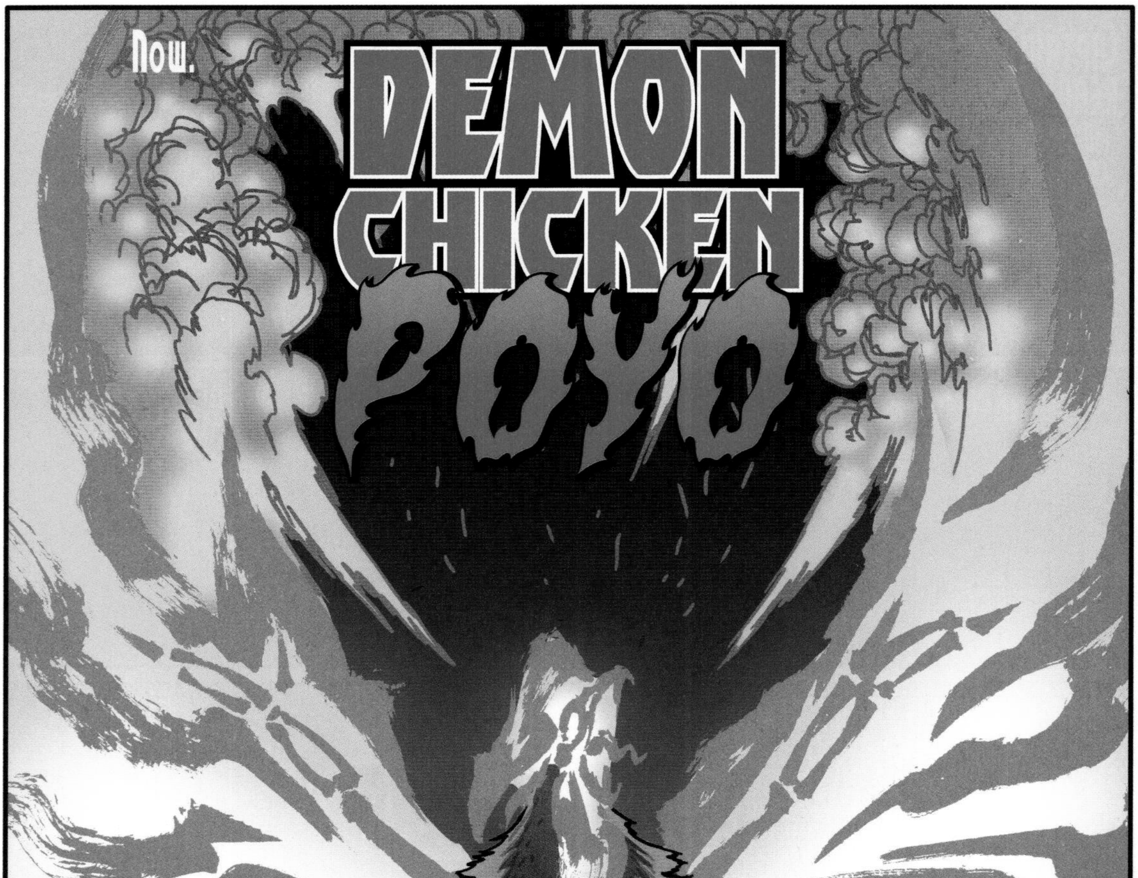
Now.
DEMON CHICKEN POYO

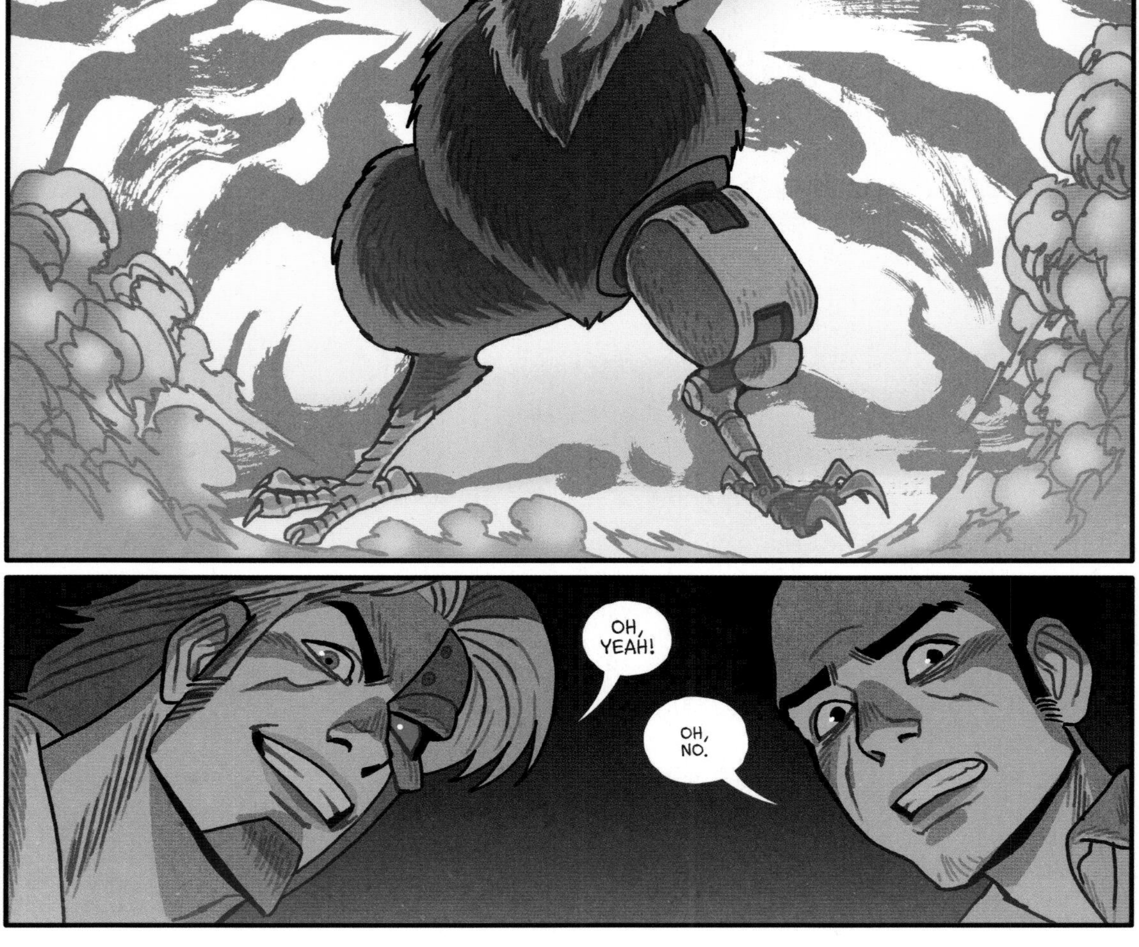
OH, YEAH!
OH, NO.

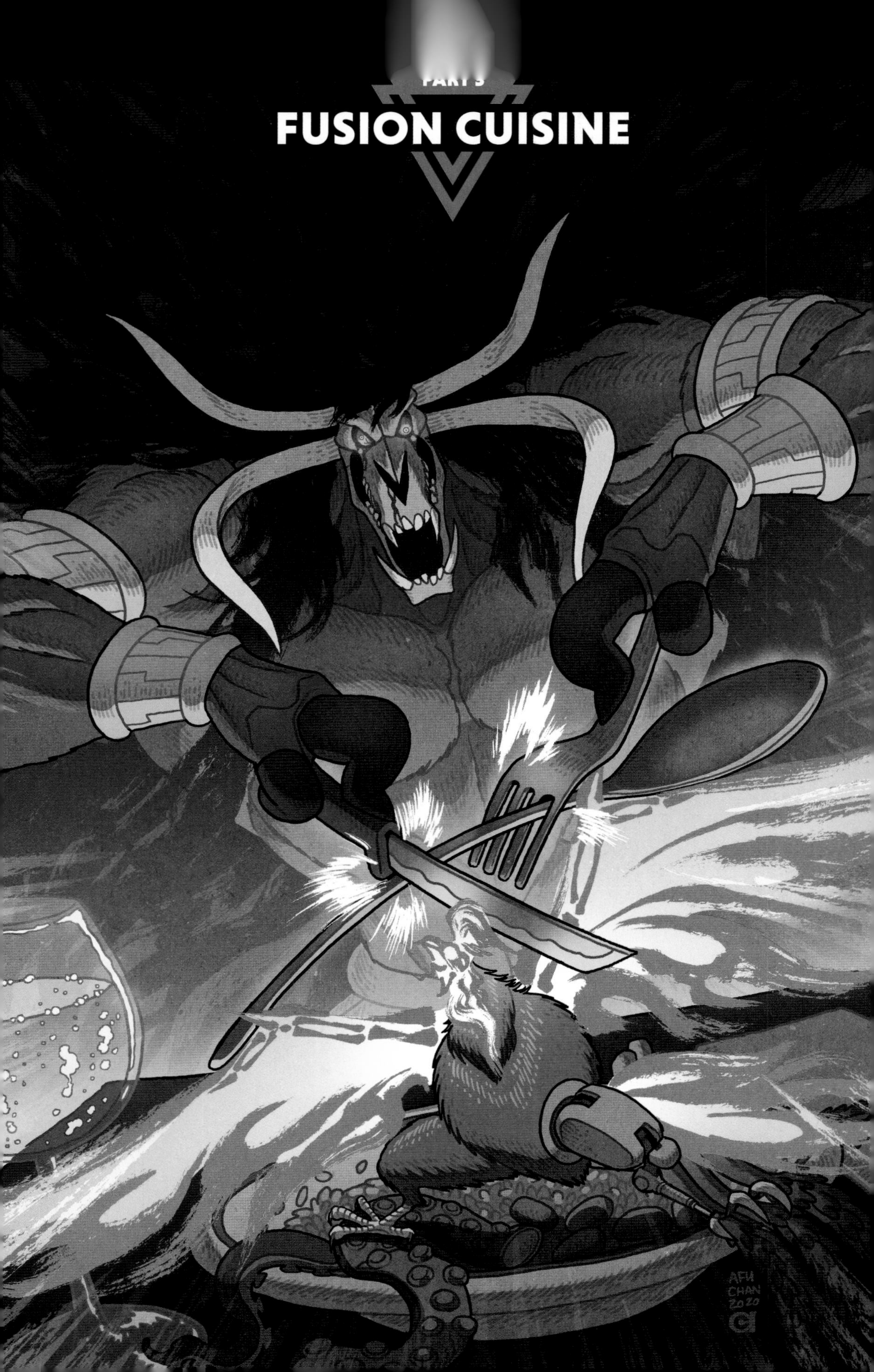
FUSION CUISINE
AFU CHAN 2020

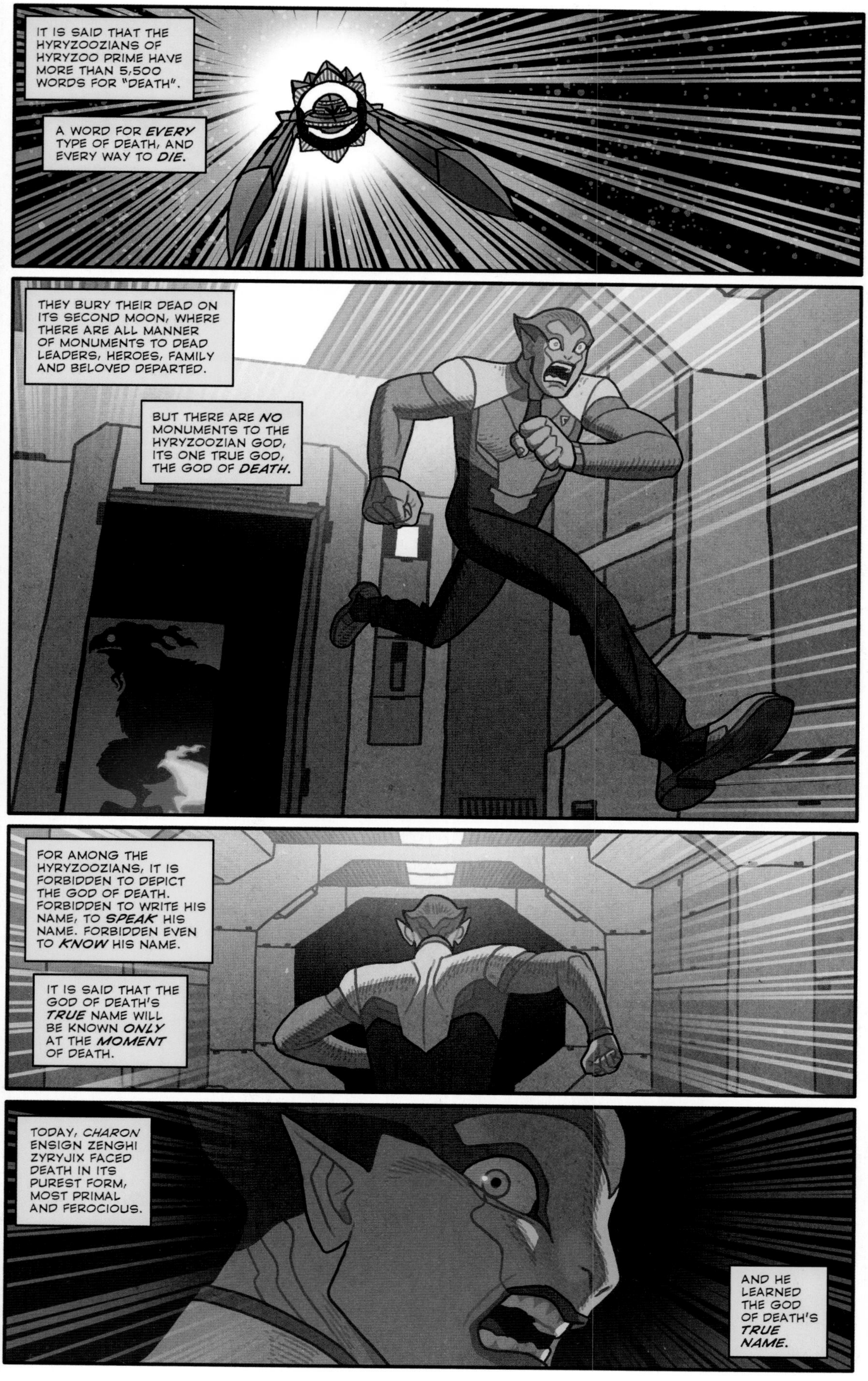
IT IS SAID THAT THE HYRYZOOZIANS OF HYRYZOO PRIME HAVE MORE THAN 5,500 WORDS FOR "DEATH".
A WORD FOR EVERY TYPE OF DEATH, AND EVERY WAY TO DIE.
THEY BURY THEIR DEAD ON ITS SECOND MOON, WHERE THERE ARE ALL MANNER OF MONUMENTS TO DEAD LEADERS, HEROES, FAMILY AND BELOVED DEPARTED.
BUT THERE ARE NO MONUMENTS TO THE HYRYZOOZIAN GOD, ITS ONE TRUE GOD, THE GOD OF DEATH.
FOR AMONG THE HYRYZOOZIANS, IT IS FORBIDDEN TO DEPICT THE GOD OF DEATH. FORBIDDEN TO WRITE HIS NAME, TO SPEAK HIS NAME. FORBIDDEN EVEN TO KNOW HIS NAME.
IT IS SAID THAT THE GOD OF DEATH'S TRUE NAME WILL BE KNOWN ONLY AT THE MOMENT OF DEATH.
TODAY, CHARON ENSIGN ZENGHI ZYRYJIX FACED DEATH IN ITS PUREST FORM, MOST PRIMAL AND FEROCIOUS.
AND HE LEARNED THE GOD OF DEATH'S TRUE NAME.

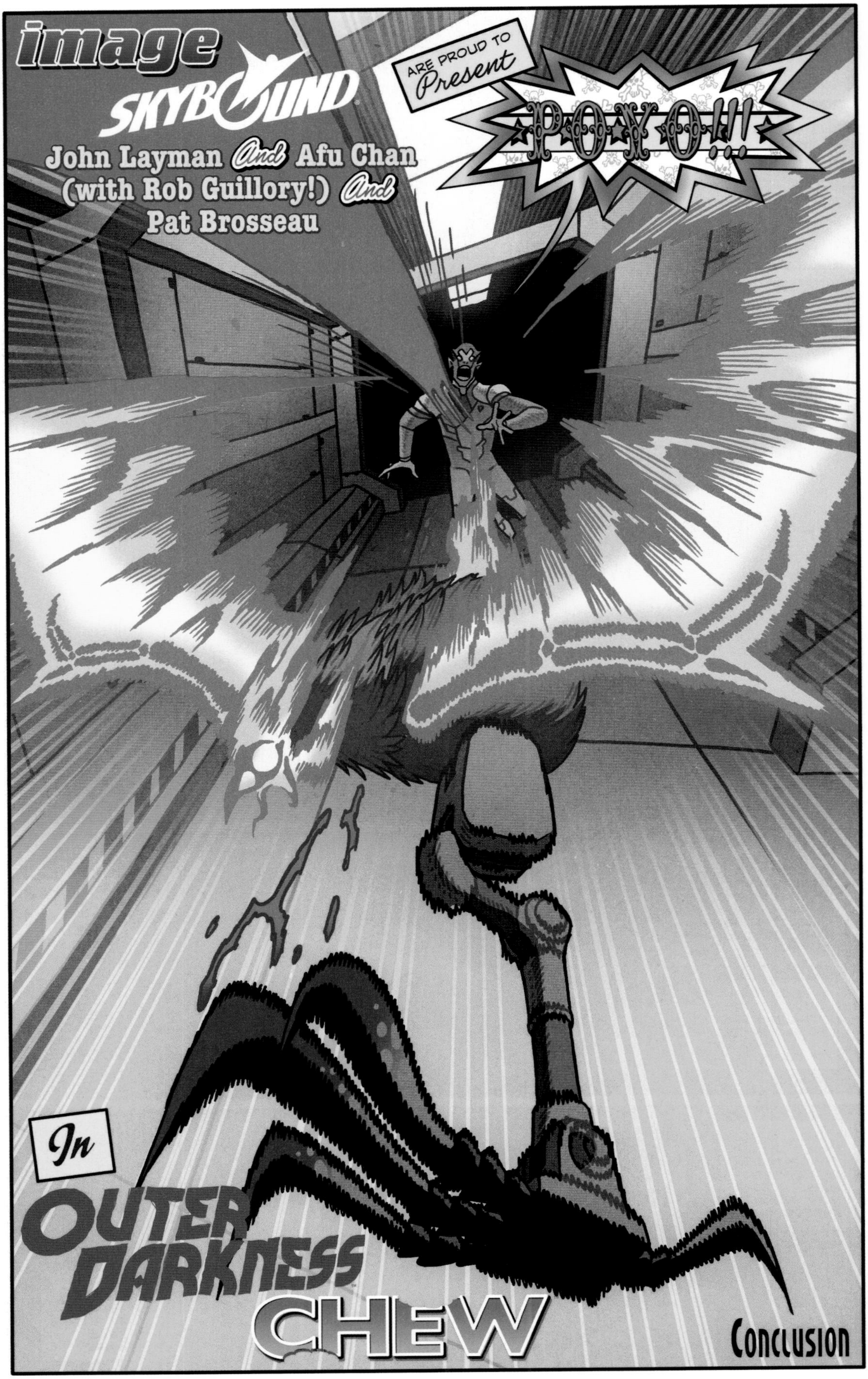
image
SKYBOUND
John Layman And Afu Chan
(with Rob Guillory!) And
Pat Brosseau
ARE PROUD TO Present
POYO!!!
In
OUTER DARKNESS
CHEW
Conclusion

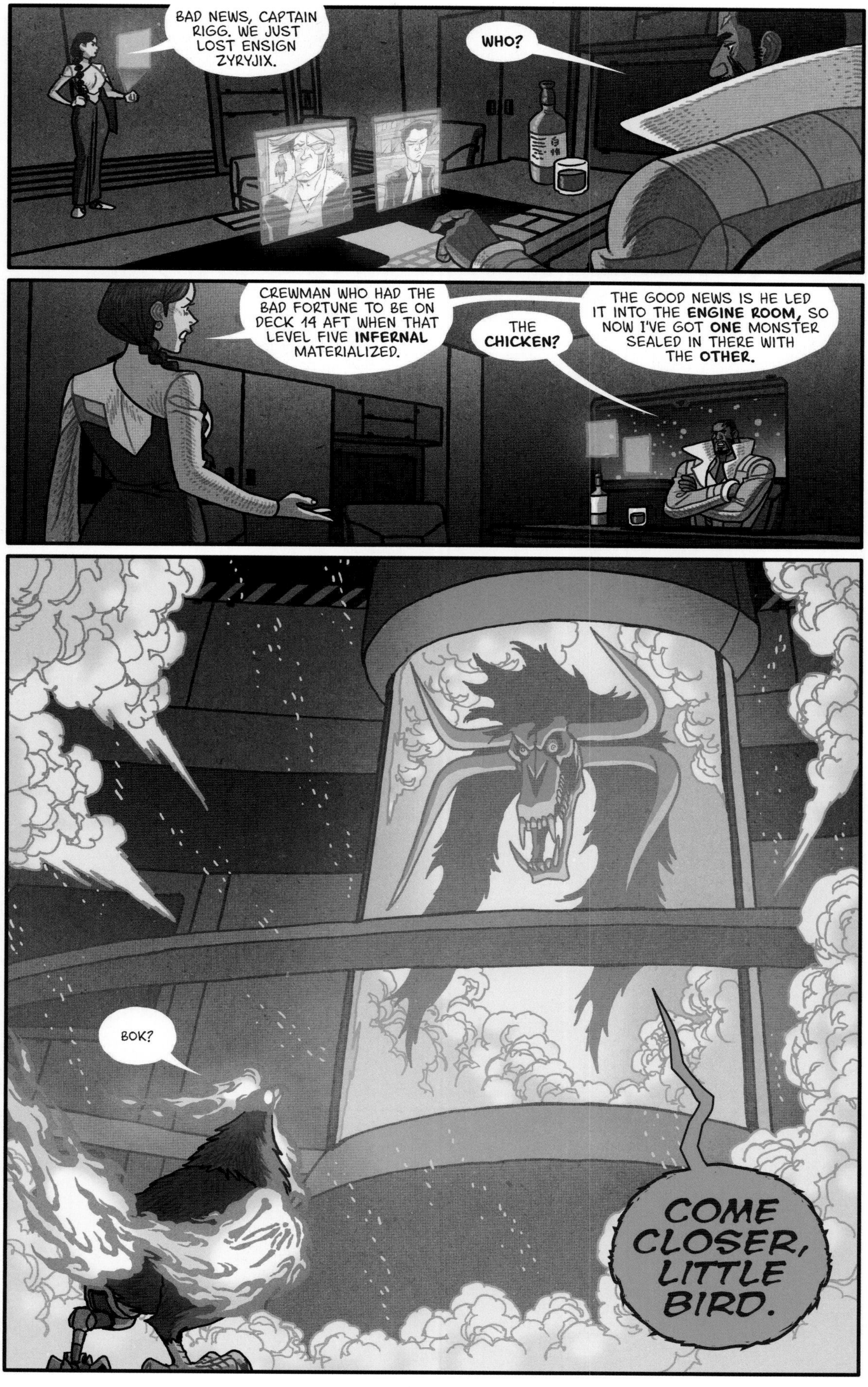
BAD NEWS, CAPTAIN RIGG. WE JUST LOST ENSIGN ZYRYJIX.
WHO?
CREWMAN WHO HAD THE BAD FORTUNE TO BE ON DECK 14 AFT WHEN THAT LEVEL FIVE INFERNAL MATERIALIZED.
THE GOOD NEWS IS HE LED IT INTO THE ENGINE ROOM, SO NOW I'VE GOT ONE MONSTER SEALED IN THERE WITH THE OTHER.
THE CHICKEN?
BOK?
COME CLOSER, LITTLE BIRD.

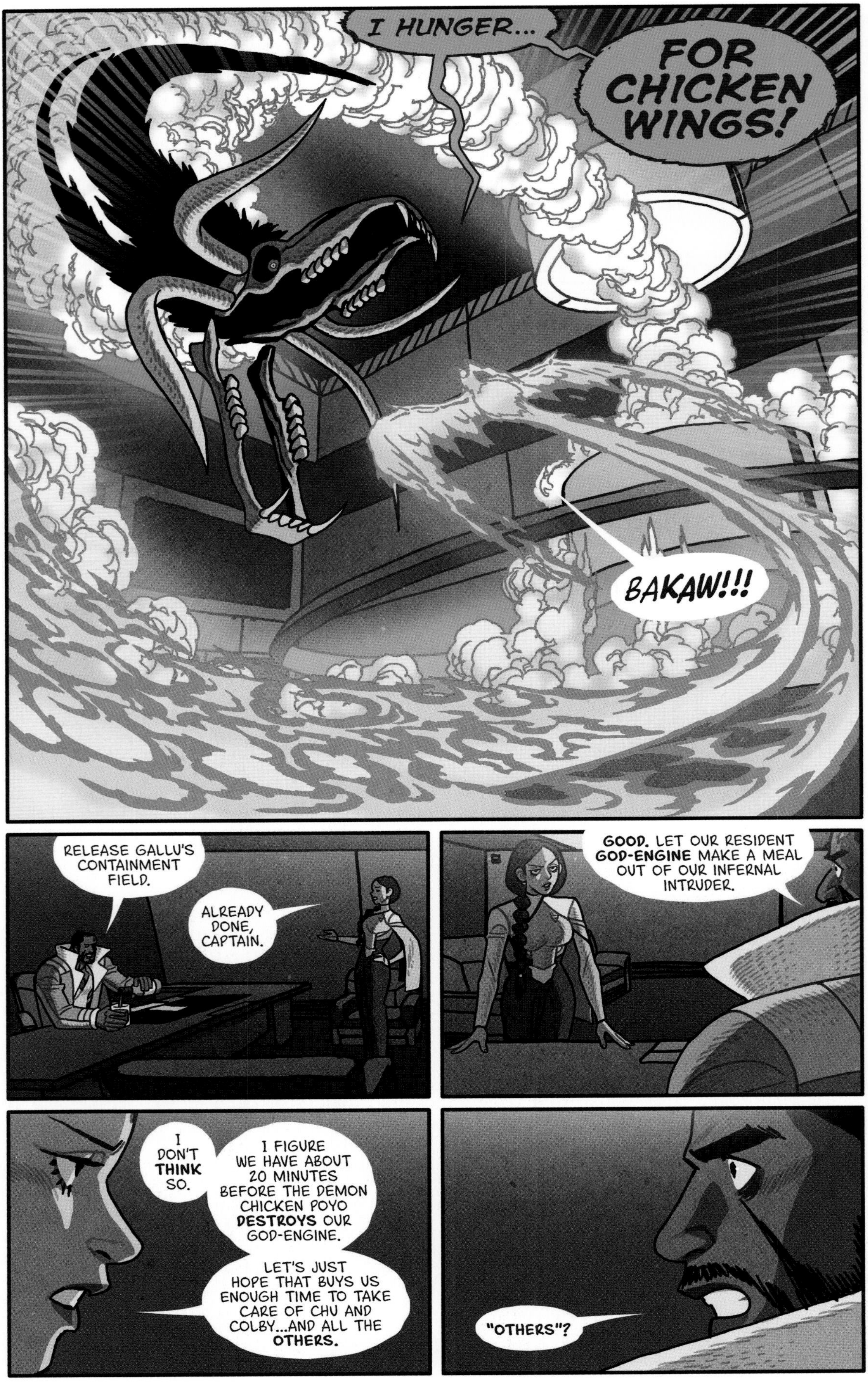
I HUNGER...
FOR CHICKEN WINGS!
BAKAW!!!
RELEASE GALLU'S CONTAINMENT FIELD.
ALREADY DONE, CAPTAIN.
GOOD. LET OUR RESIDENT **GOD-ENGINE** MAKE A MEAL OUT OF OUR INFERNAL INTRUDER.
I DON'T **THINK** SO.
I FIGURE WE HAVE ABOUT 20 MINUTES BEFORE THE DEMON CHICKEN POYO **DESTROYS** OUR GOD-ENGINE.
LET'S JUST HOPE THAT BUYS US ENOUGH TIME TO TAKE CARE OF CHU AND COLBY...AND ALL THE **OTHERS.**
"OTHERS"?

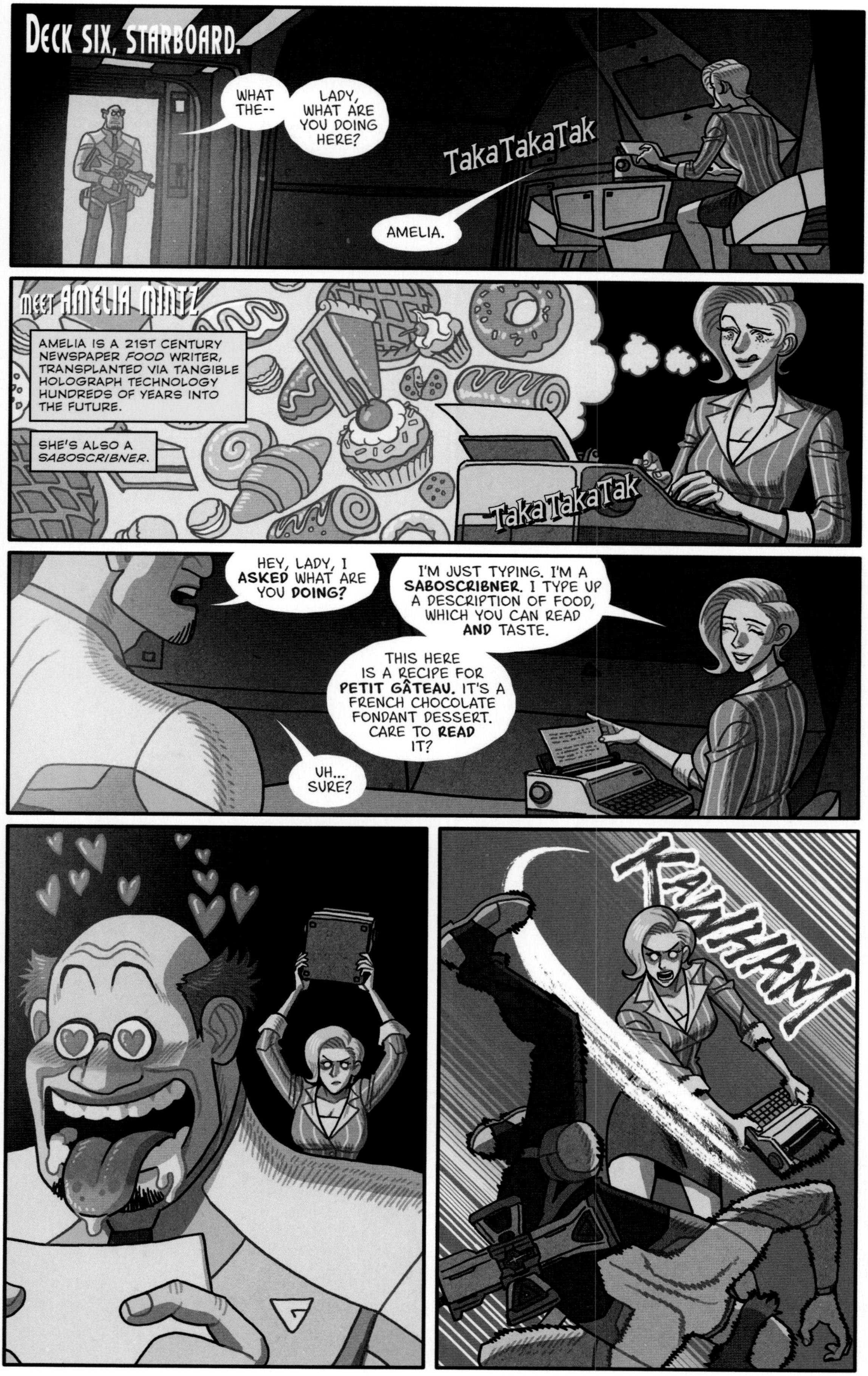
Deck six, starboard.
WHAT THE--
LADY, WHAT ARE YOU DOING HERE?
TakaTakaTak
AMELIA.
meet AMELIA MINTZ
AMELIA IS A 21ST CENTURY NEWSPAPER FOOD WRITER, TRANSPLANTED VIA TANGIBLE HOLOGRAPH TECHNOLOGY HUNDREDS OF YEARS INTO THE FUTURE.
SHE'S ALSO A SABOSCRIBNER.
TakaTakaTak
HEY, LADY, I ASKED WHAT ARE YOU DOING?
I'M JUST TYPING. I'M A SABOSCRIBNER. I TYPE UP A DESCRIPTION OF FOOD, WHICH YOU CAN READ AND TASTE.
THIS HERE IS A RECIPE FOR PETIT GÂTEAU. IT'S A FRENCH CHOCOLATE FONDANT DESSERT. CARE TO READ IT?
UH... SURE?
KAWHAM

ELSEWHERE: MEET MASON SAVOY

YOU'RE NOT SUPPOSED TO **BE** HERE, BIG FELLA.

OH, DON'T MIND ME, MY GOOD MAN. I'M JUST ENJOYING A PLEASANT EVENING PERAMBULATION AND CONSTITUTIONAL BEFORE THE **FESTIVITIES** GET UNDERWAY.

"FESTIVITIES"?

RED ALERT! THIS IS THE CAPTAIN. LOOKS LIKE WE'RE DEALING WITH AN INCURSION OF THE HOLOGRAPHICALLY **POSSESSED**--AND IT'S STARTING TO **SPREAD**.

GRAB YOUR SPELL BOOKS AND GUNS, AND GET READY FOR A FIGHT.

KLOOOCH

FESTIVITIES!

RED ALERT!

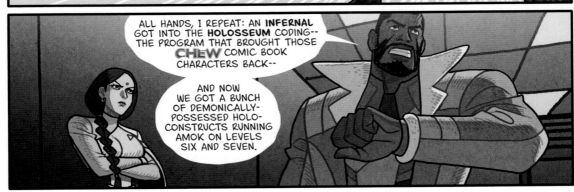

ALL HANDS, I REPEAT: AN **INFERNAL** GOT INTO THE **HOLOSSEUM** CODING-- THE PROGRAM THAT BROUGHT THOSE **CHEW** COMIC BOOK CHARACTERS BACK--

AND NOW WE GOT A BUNCH OF DEMONICALLY- POSSESSED HOLO- CONSTRUCTS RUNNING AMOK ON LEVELS SIX AND SEVEN.

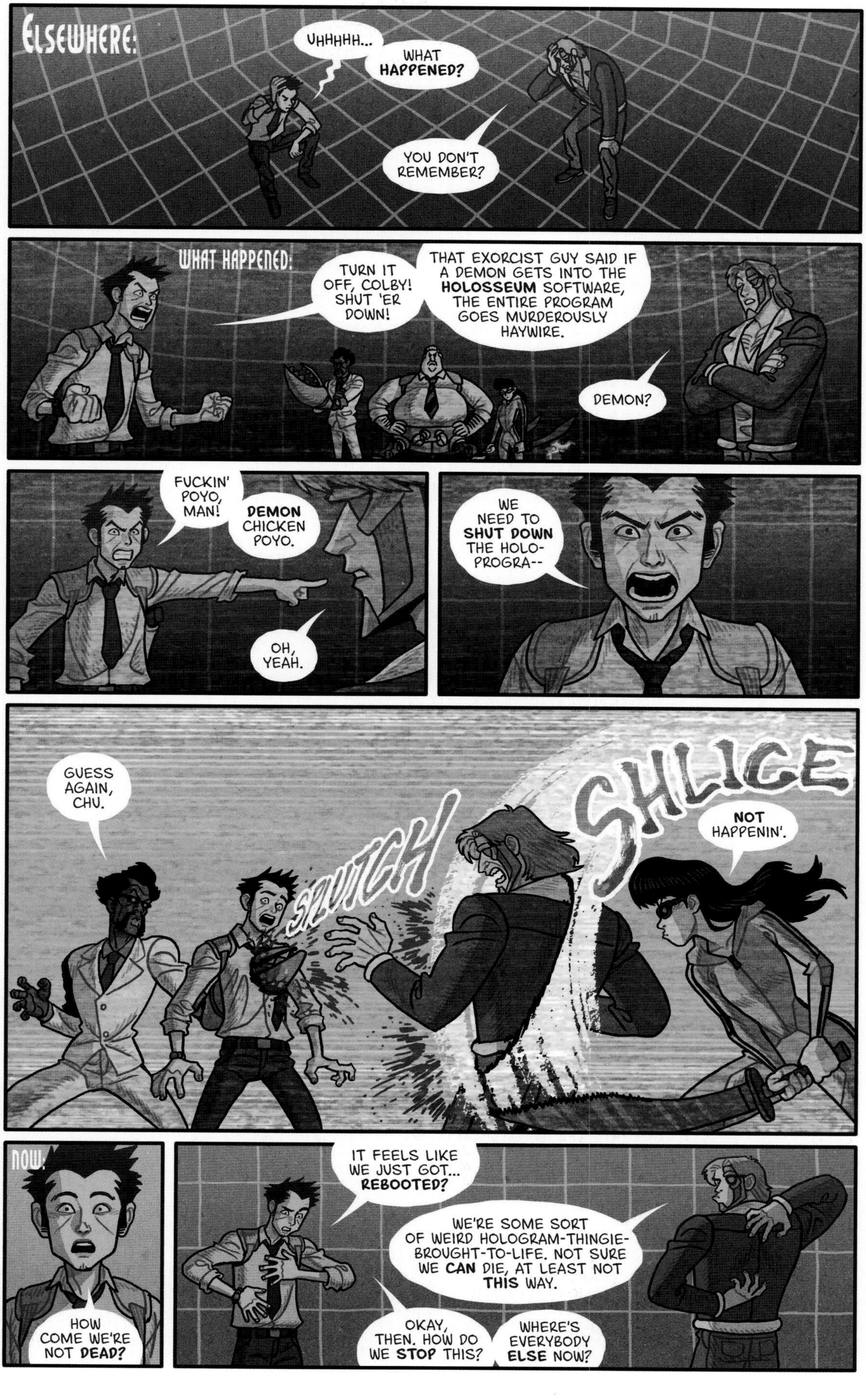
ELSEWHERE:
UHHHHH...
WHAT HAPPENED?
YOU DON'T REMEMBER?
WHAT HAPPENED:
TURN IT OFF, COLBY! SHUT 'ER DOWN!
THAT EXORCIST GUY SAID IF A DEMON GETS INTO THE HOLOSSEUM SOFTWARE, THE ENTIRE PROGRAM GOES MURDEROUSLY HAYWIRE.
DEMON?
FUCKIN' POYO, MAN!
DEMON CHICKEN POYO.
OH, YEAH.
WE NEED TO SHUT DOWN THE HOLO-PROGRA--
GUESS AGAIN, CHU.
SPLUTCH
SHLICE
NOT HAPPENIN'.
NOW:
HOW COME WE'RE NOT DEAD?
IT FEELS LIKE WE JUST GOT... REBOOTED?
WE'RE SOME SORT OF WEIRD HOLOGRAM-THINGIE-BROUGHT-TO-LIFE. NOT SURE WE CAN DIE, AT LEAST NOT THIS WAY.
OKAY, THEN. HOW DO WE STOP THIS?
WHERE'S EVERYBODY ELSE NOW?

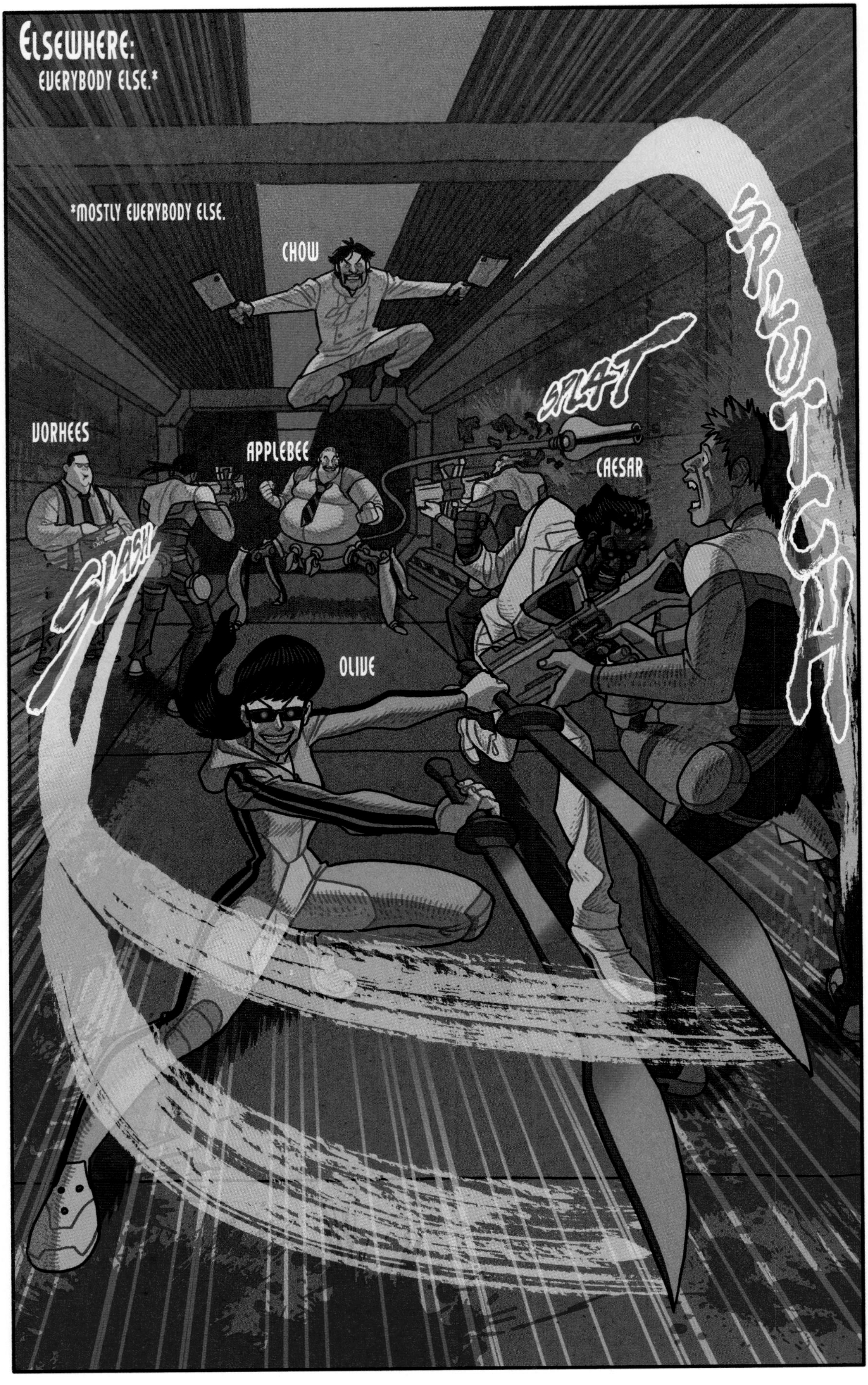
ELSEWHERE:
EVERYBODY ELSE.*
*MOSTLY EVERYBODY ELSE.
CHOW
VORHEES
APPLEBEE
CAESAR
OLIVE
SPLAT
SLASH
SKLUTCH

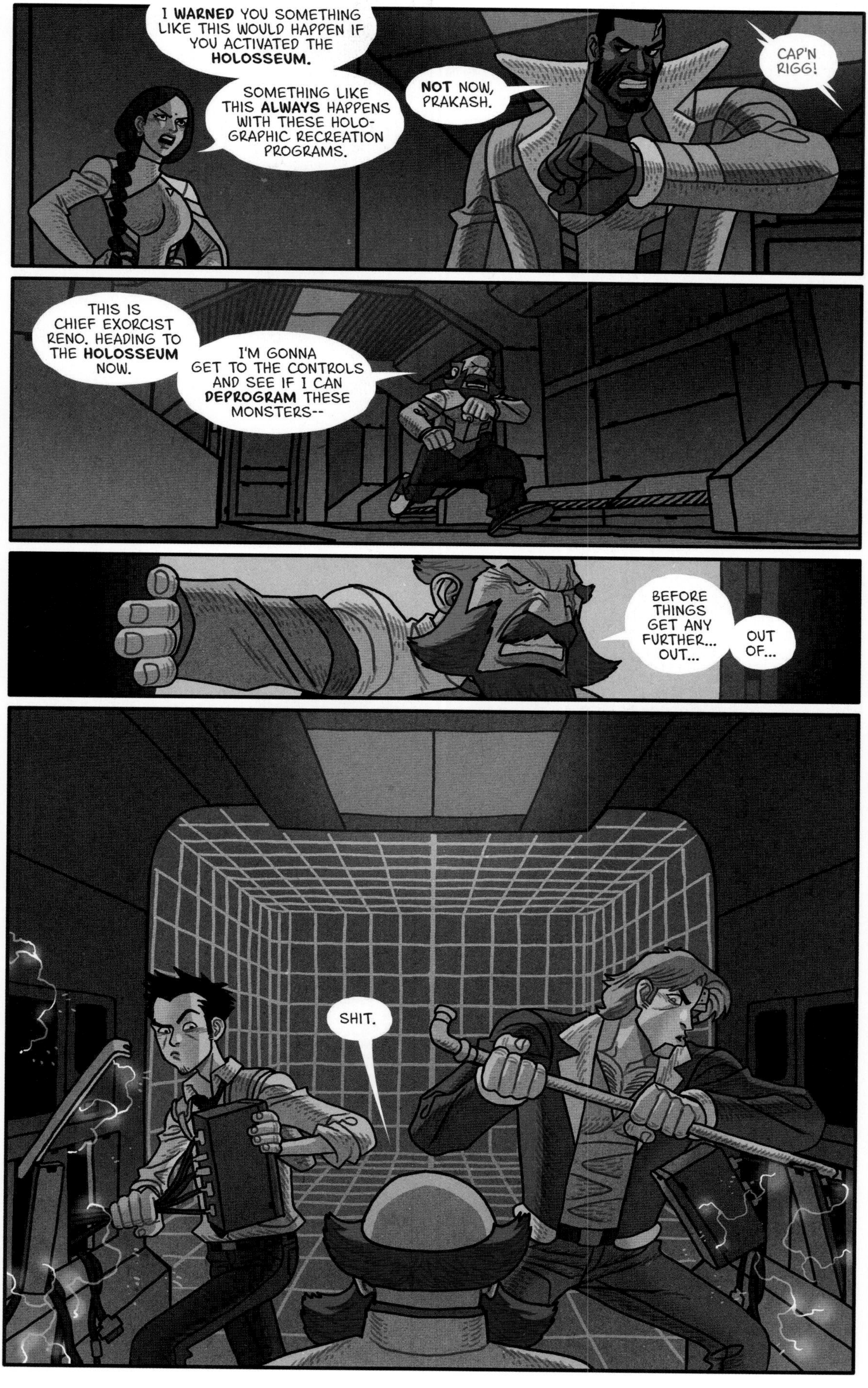
I **WARNED** YOU SOMETHING LIKE THIS WOULD HAPPEN IF YOU ACTIVATED THE **HOLOSSEUM.**
SOMETHING LIKE THIS **ALWAYS** HAPPENS WITH THESE HOLO-GRAPHIC RECREATION PROGRAMS.
NOT NOW, PRAKASH.
CAP'N RIGG!
THIS IS CHIEF EXORCIST RENO. HEADING TO THE **HOLOSSEUM** NOW.
I'M GONNA GET TO THE CONTROLS AND SEE IF I CAN **DEPROGRAM** THESE MONSTERS--
BEFORE THINGS GET ANY FURTHER... OUT...
OUT OF...
SHIT.

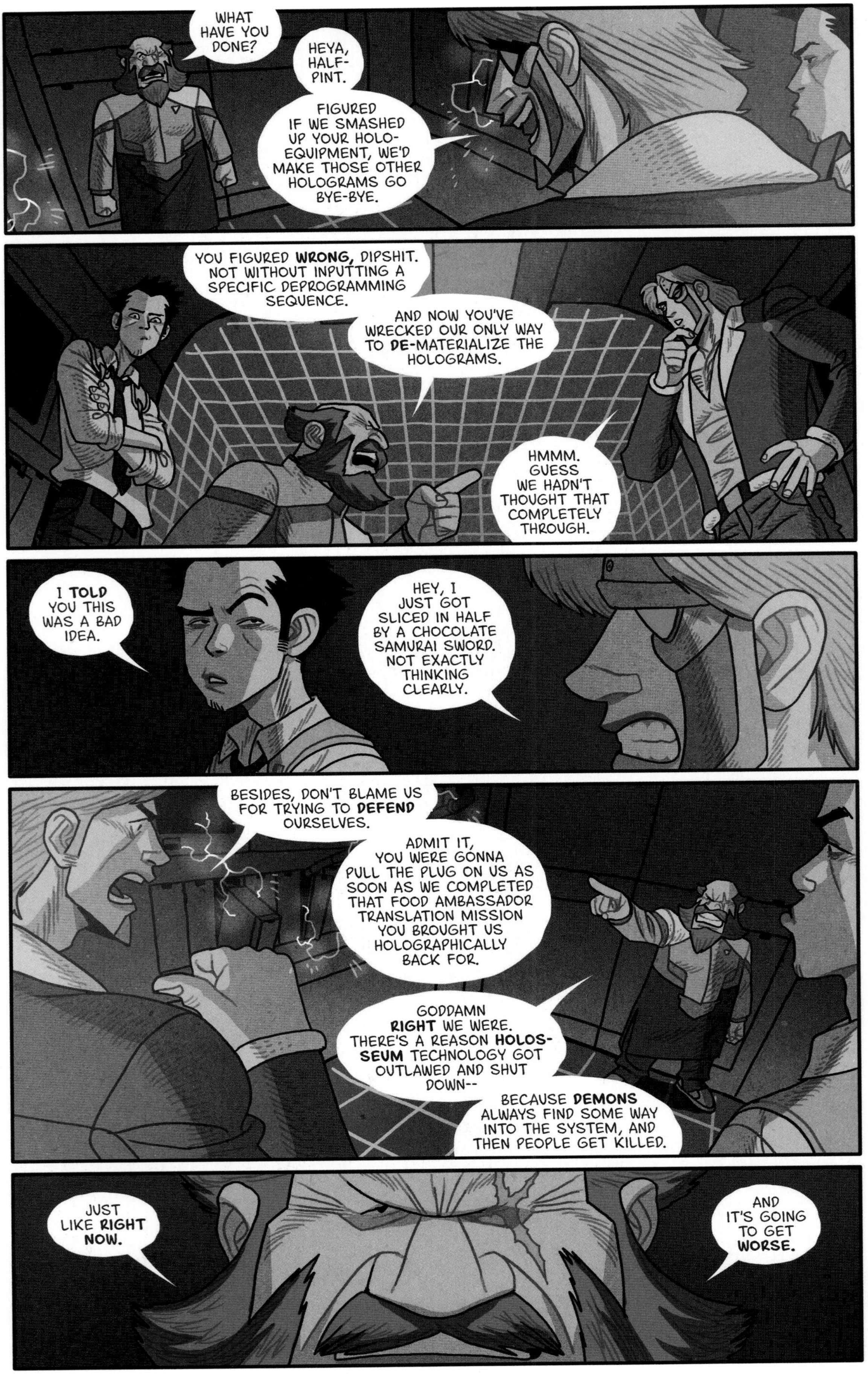
WHAT HAVE YOU DONE?
HEYA, HALF-PINT.
FIGURED IF WE SMASHED UP YOUR HOLO-EQUIPMENT, WE'D MAKE THOSE OTHER HOLOGRAMS GO BYE-BYE.
YOU FIGURED **WRONG,** DIPSHIT. NOT WITHOUT INPUTTING A SPECIFIC DEPROGRAMMING SEQUENCE.
AND NOW YOU'VE WRECKED OUR ONLY WAY TO **DE-**MATERIALIZE THE HOLOGRAMS.
HMMM. GUESS WE HADN'T THOUGHT THAT COMPLETELY THROUGH.
I **TOLD** YOU THIS WAS A BAD IDEA.
HEY, I JUST GOT SLICED IN HALF BY A CHOCOLATE SAMURAI SWORD. NOT EXACTLY THINKING CLEARLY.
BESIDES, DON'T BLAME US FOR TRYING TO **DEFEND** OURSELVES.
ADMIT IT, YOU WERE GONNA PULL THE PLUG ON US AS SOON AS WE COMPLETED THAT FOOD AMBASSADOR TRANSLATION MISSION YOU BROUGHT US HOLOGRAPHICALLY BACK FOR.
GODDAMN **RIGHT** WE WERE. THERE'S A REASON **HOLOS-SEUM** TECHNOLOGY GOT OUTLAWED AND SHUT DOWN--
BECAUSE **DEMONS** ALWAYS FIND SOME WAY INTO THE SYSTEM, AND THEN PEOPLE GET KILLED.
JUST LIKE **RIGHT NOW.**
AND IT'S GOING TO GET **WORSE.**

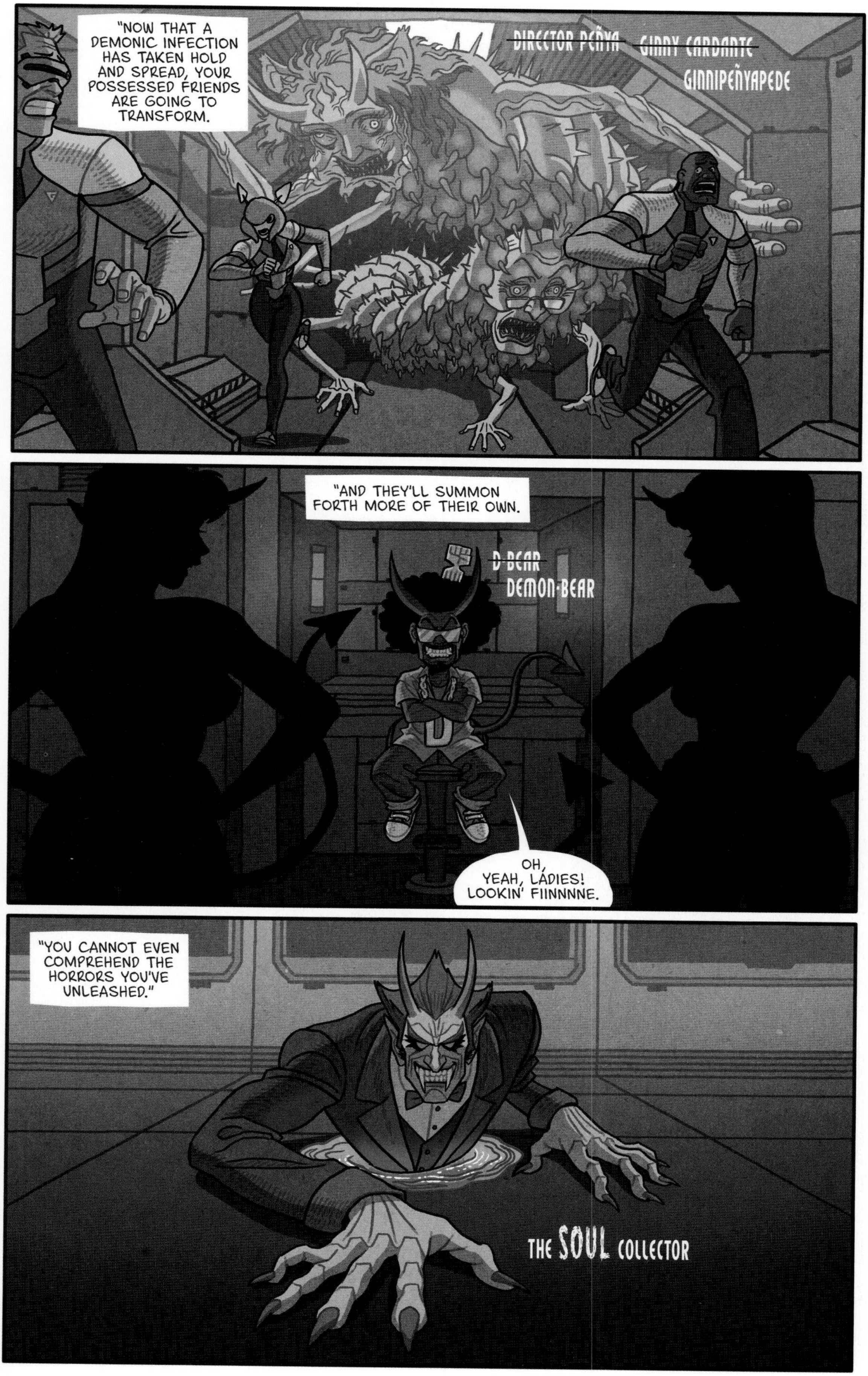
"NOW THAT A DEMONIC INFECTION HAS TAKEN HOLD AND SPREAD, YOUR POSSESSED FRIENDS ARE GOING TO TRANSFORM.
DIRECTOR PEÑYA GINNY CARDANTE
GINNIPEÑYAPEDE
"AND THEY'LL SUMMON FORTH MORE OF THEIR OWN.
D-BEAR
DEMON-BEAR
OH, YEAH, LADIES! LOOKIN' FIINNNNE.
"YOU CANNOT EVEN COMPREHEND THE HORRORS YOU'VE UNLEASHED."
THE SOUL COLLECTOR

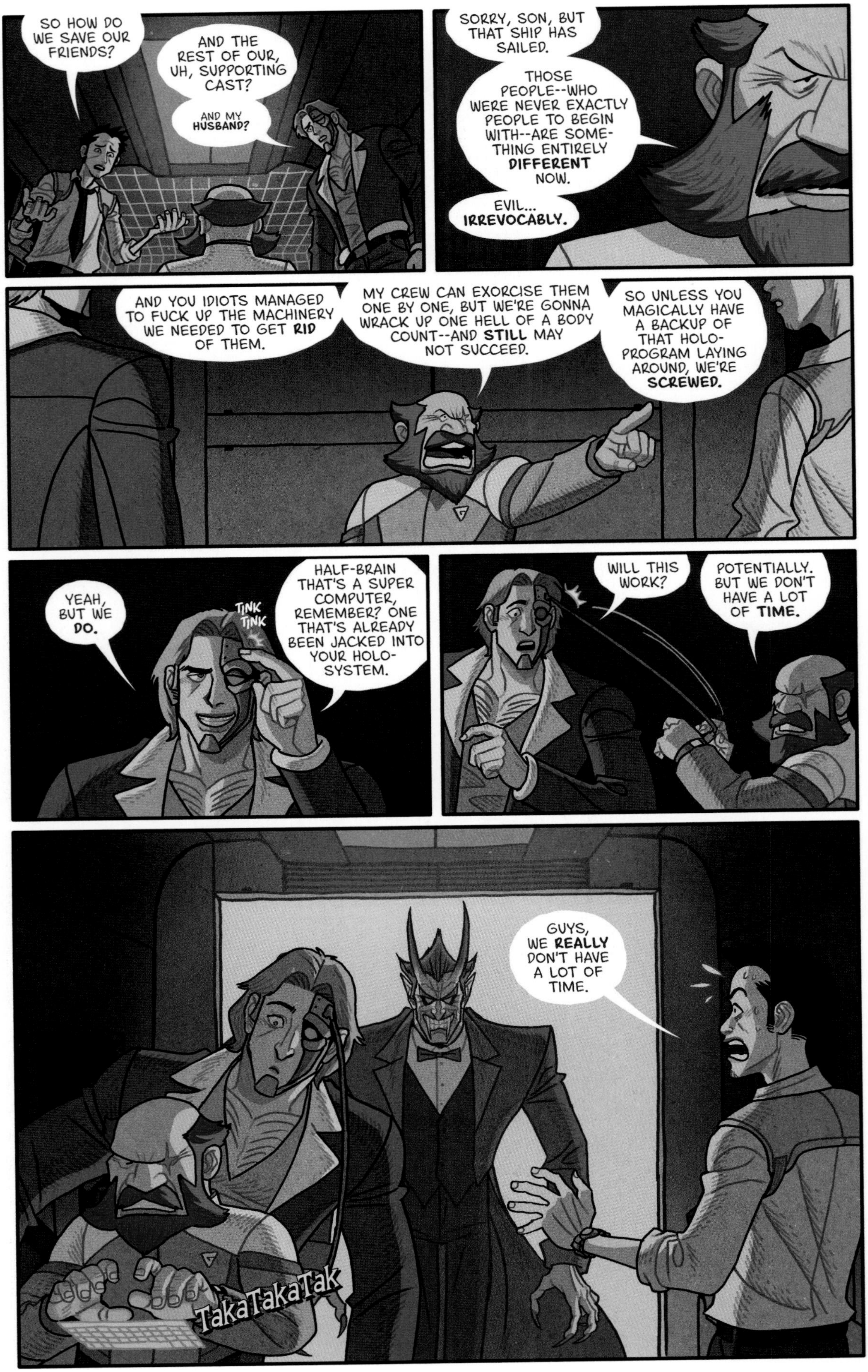
SO HOW DO WE SAVE OUR FRIENDS?
AND THE REST OF OUR, UH, SUPPORTING CAST?
AND MY HUSBAND?
SORRY, SON, BUT THAT SHIP HAS SAILED.
THOSE PEOPLE--WHO WERE NEVER EXACTLY PEOPLE TO BEGIN WITH--ARE SOMETHING ENTIRELY DIFFERENT NOW.
EVIL... IRREVOCABLY.
AND YOU IDIOTS MANAGED TO FUCK UP THE MACHINERY WE NEEDED TO GET RID OF THEM.
MY CREW CAN EXORCISE THEM ONE BY ONE, BUT WE'RE GONNA WRACK UP ONE HELL OF A BODY COUNT--AND STILL MAY NOT SUCCEED.
SO UNLESS YOU MAGICALLY HAVE A BACKUP OF THAT HOLO-PROGRAM LAYING AROUND, WE'RE SCREWED.
YEAH, BUT WE DO.
TINK TINK
HALF-BRAIN THAT'S A SUPER COMPUTER, REMEMBER? ONE THAT'S ALREADY BEEN JACKED INTO YOUR HOLO-SYSTEM.
WILL THIS WORK?
POTENTIALLY. BUT WE DON'T HAVE A LOT OF TIME.
GUYS, WE REALLY DON'T HAVE A LOT OF TIME.
TakaTakaTak

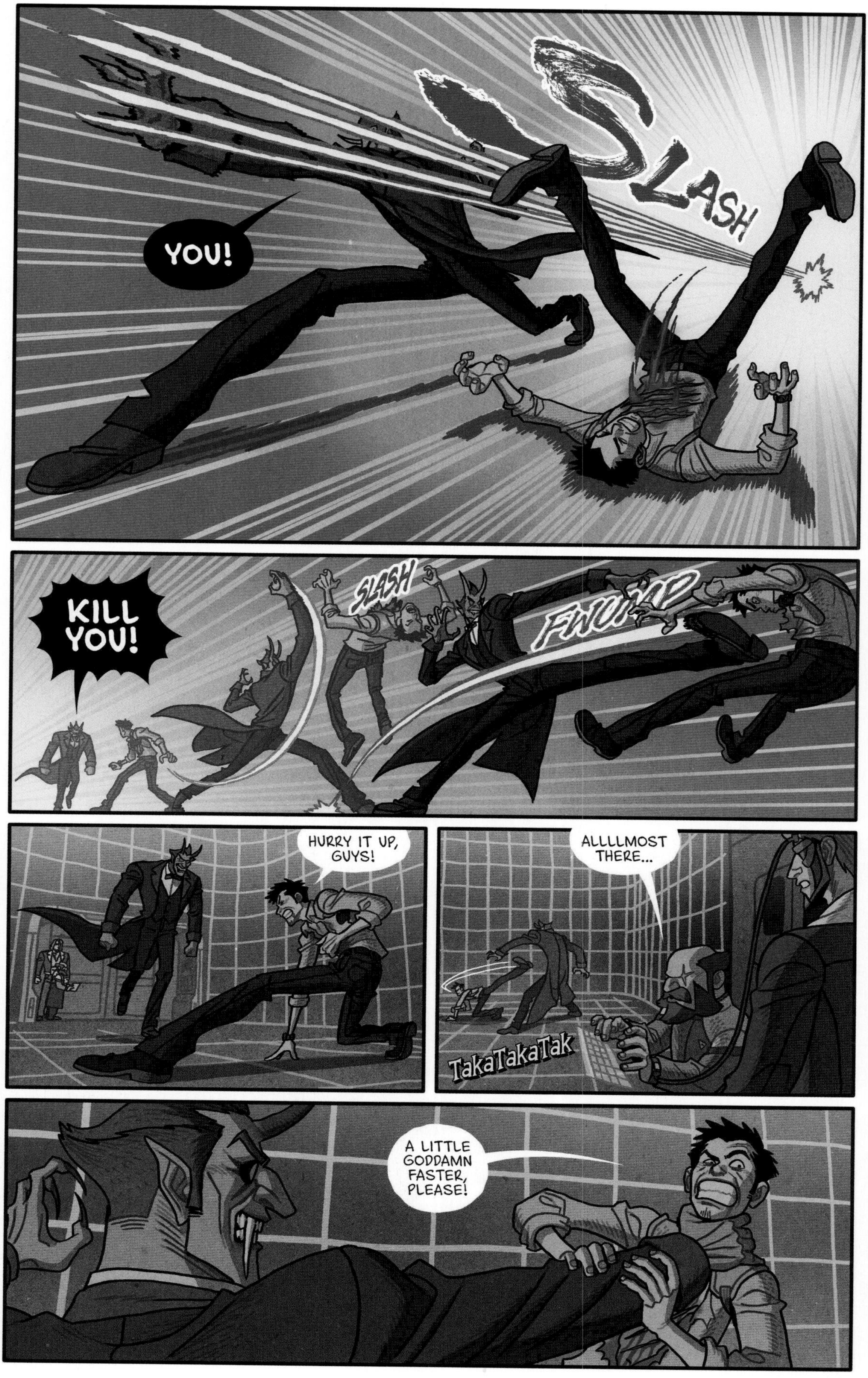
SLASH
YOU!
KILL YOU!
SLASH
FWOMP
HURRY IT UP, GUYS!
ALLLLMOST THERE...
TakaTakaTak
A LITTLE GODDAMN FASTER, PLEASE!

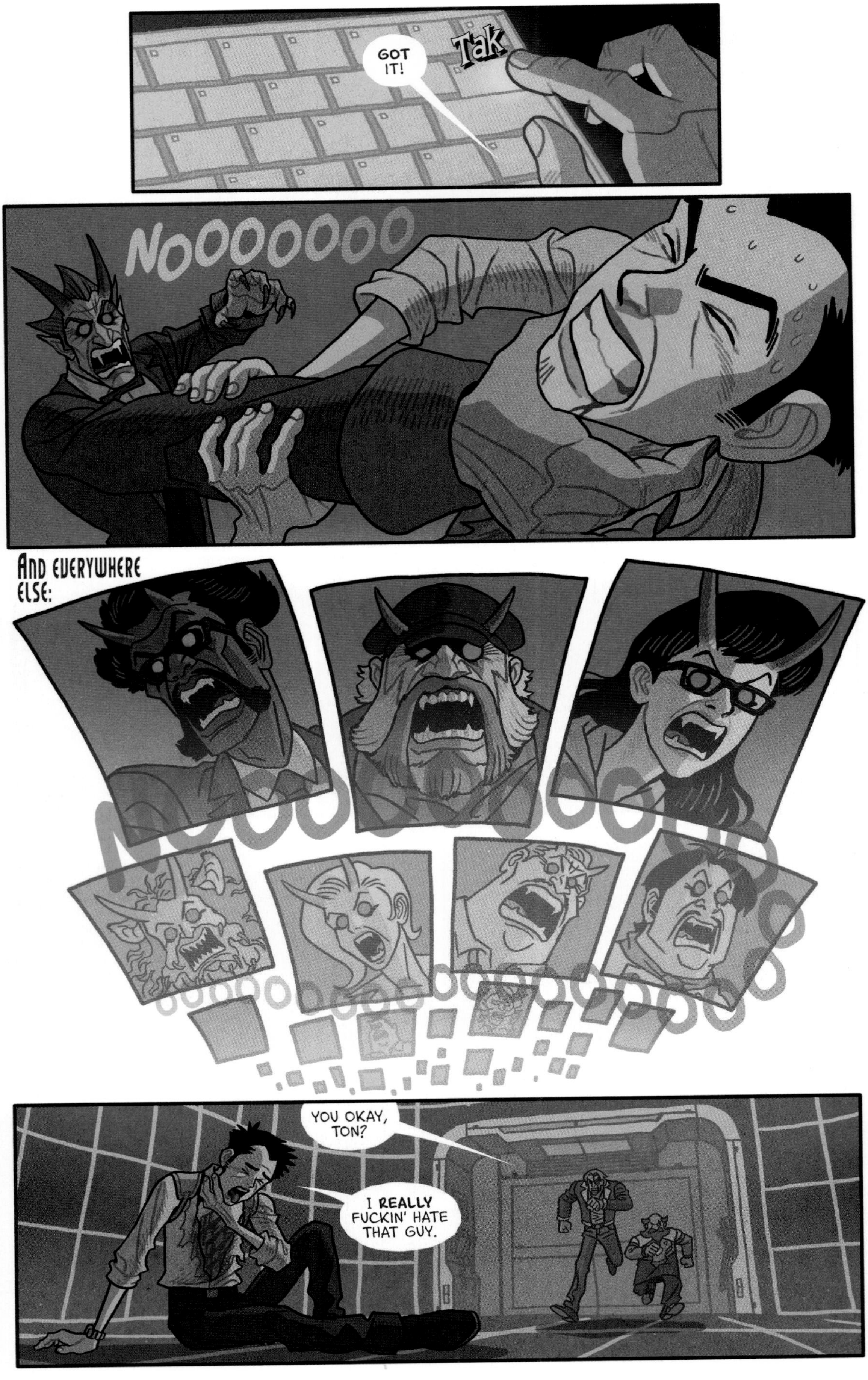
GOT IT!
TAK
NOOOOOOO
AND EVERYWHERE ELSE:
YOU OKAY, TON?
I REALLY FUCKIN' HATE THAT GUY.

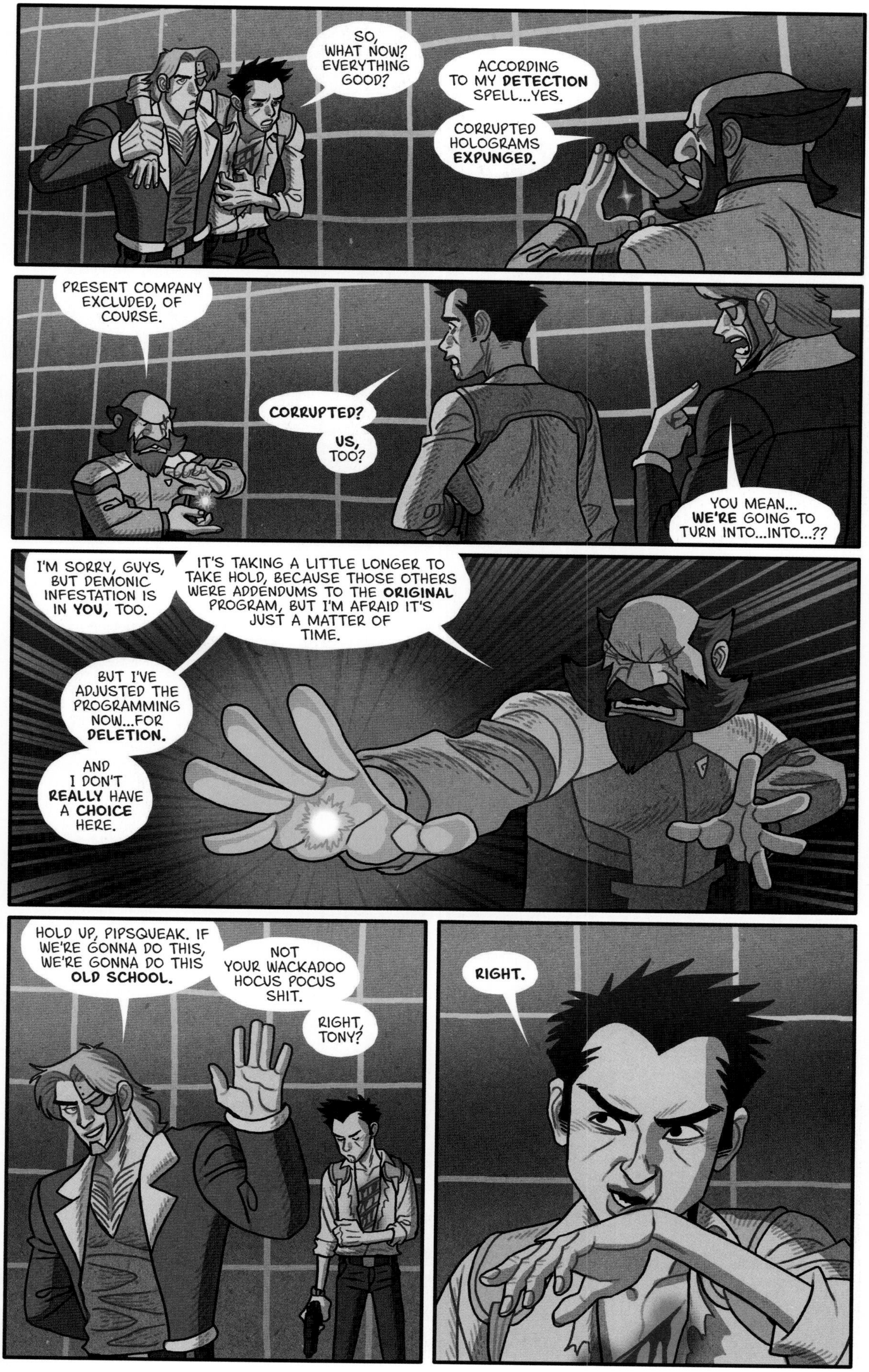
SO, WHAT NOW? EVERYTHING GOOD?
ACCORDING TO MY **DETECTION** SPELL...YES.
CORRUPTED HOLOGRAMS **EXPUNGED.**
PRESENT COMPANY EXCLUDED, OF COURSE.
CORRUPTED?
US, TOO?
YOU MEAN... **WE'RE** GOING TO TURN INTO...INTO...??
I'M SORRY, GUYS, BUT DEMONIC INFESTATION IS IN **YOU,** TOO.
IT'S TAKING A LITTLE LONGER TO TAKE HOLD, BECAUSE THOSE OTHERS WERE ADDENDUMS TO THE **ORIGINAL** PROGRAM, BUT I'M AFRAID IT'S JUST A MATTER OF TIME.
BUT I'VE ADJUSTED THE PROGRAMMING NOW...FOR **DELETION.**
AND I DON'T **REALLY** HAVE A **CHOICE** HERE.
HOLD UP, PIPSQUEAK. IF WE'RE GONNA DO THIS, WE'RE GONNA DO THIS **OLD SCHOOL.**
NOT YOUR WACKADOO HOCUS POCUS SHIT.
RIGHT, TONY?
RIGHT.

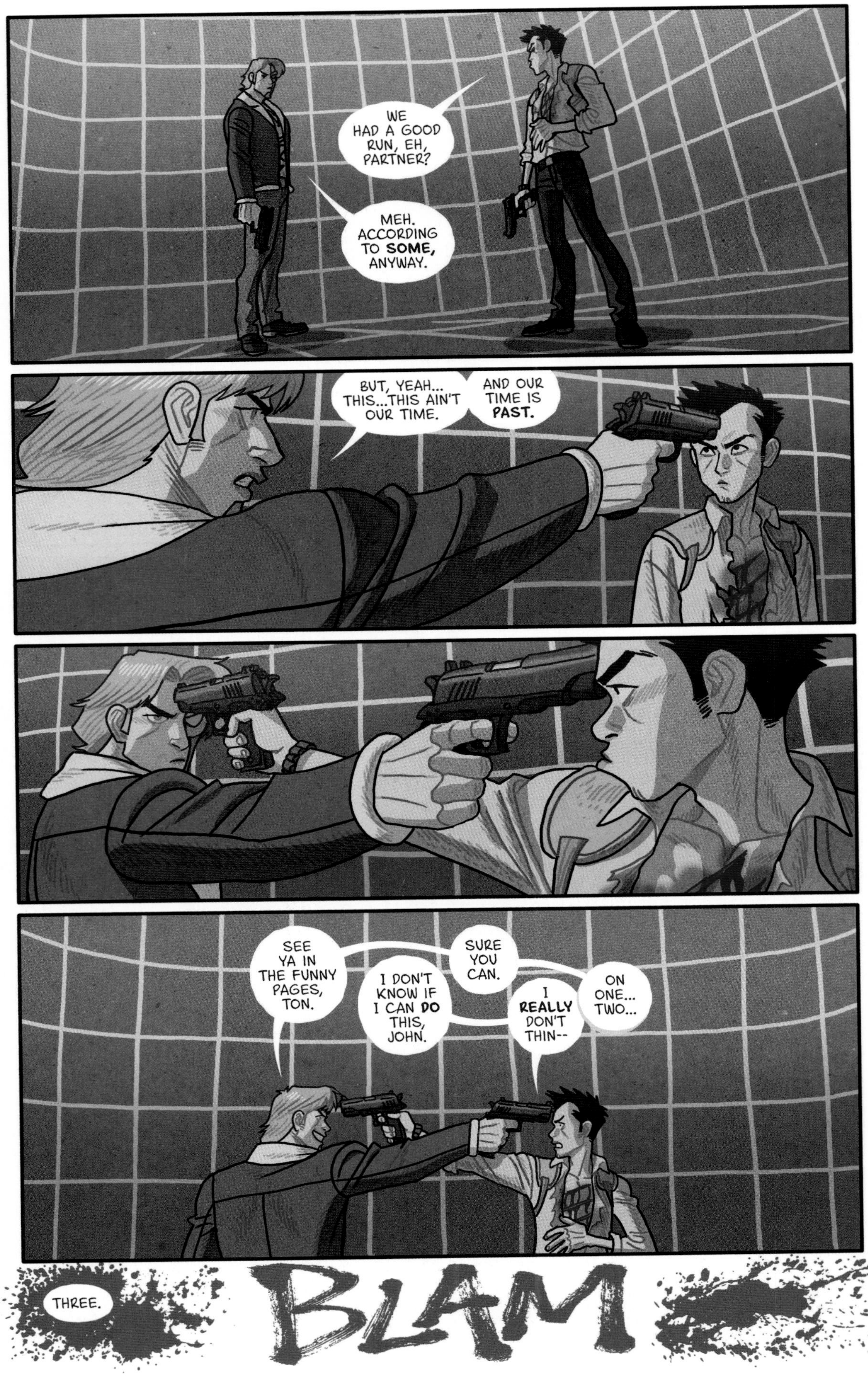
WE HAD A GOOD RUN, EH, PARTNER?
MEH. ACCORDING TO **SOME,** ANYWAY.
BUT, YEAH... THIS...THIS AIN'T OUR TIME.
AND OUR TIME IS **PAST.**
SEE YA IN THE FUNNY PAGES, TON.
I DON'T KNOW IF I CAN **DO** THIS, JOHN.
SURE YOU CAN.
I **REALLY** DON'T THIN--
ON ONE... TWO...
THREE.
BLAM

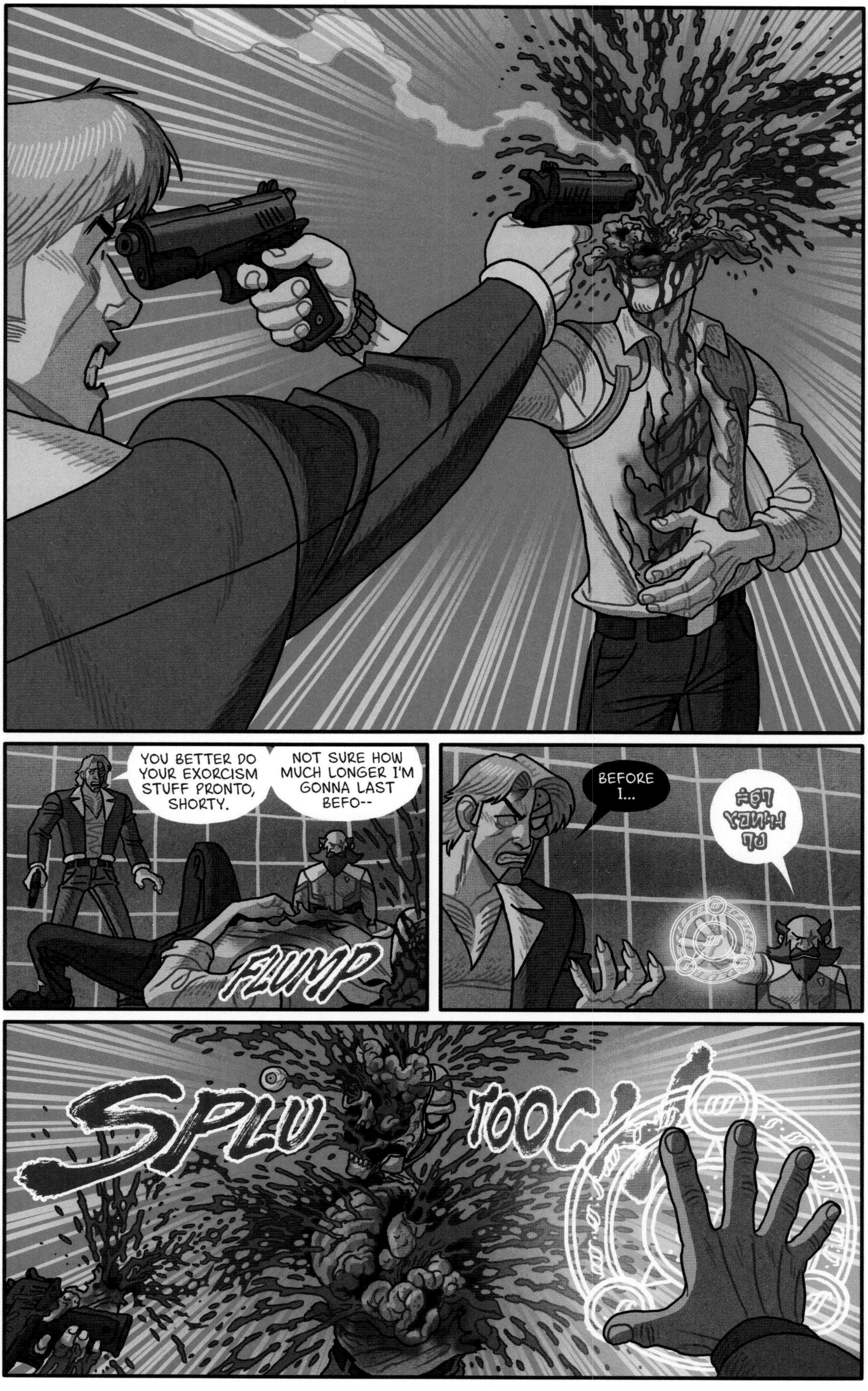
YOU BETTER DO YOUR EXORCISM STUFF PRONTO, SHORTY.
NOT SURE HOW MUCH LONGER I'M GONNA LAST BEFO--
FLUMP
BEFORE I...
SPLU TOOC!!

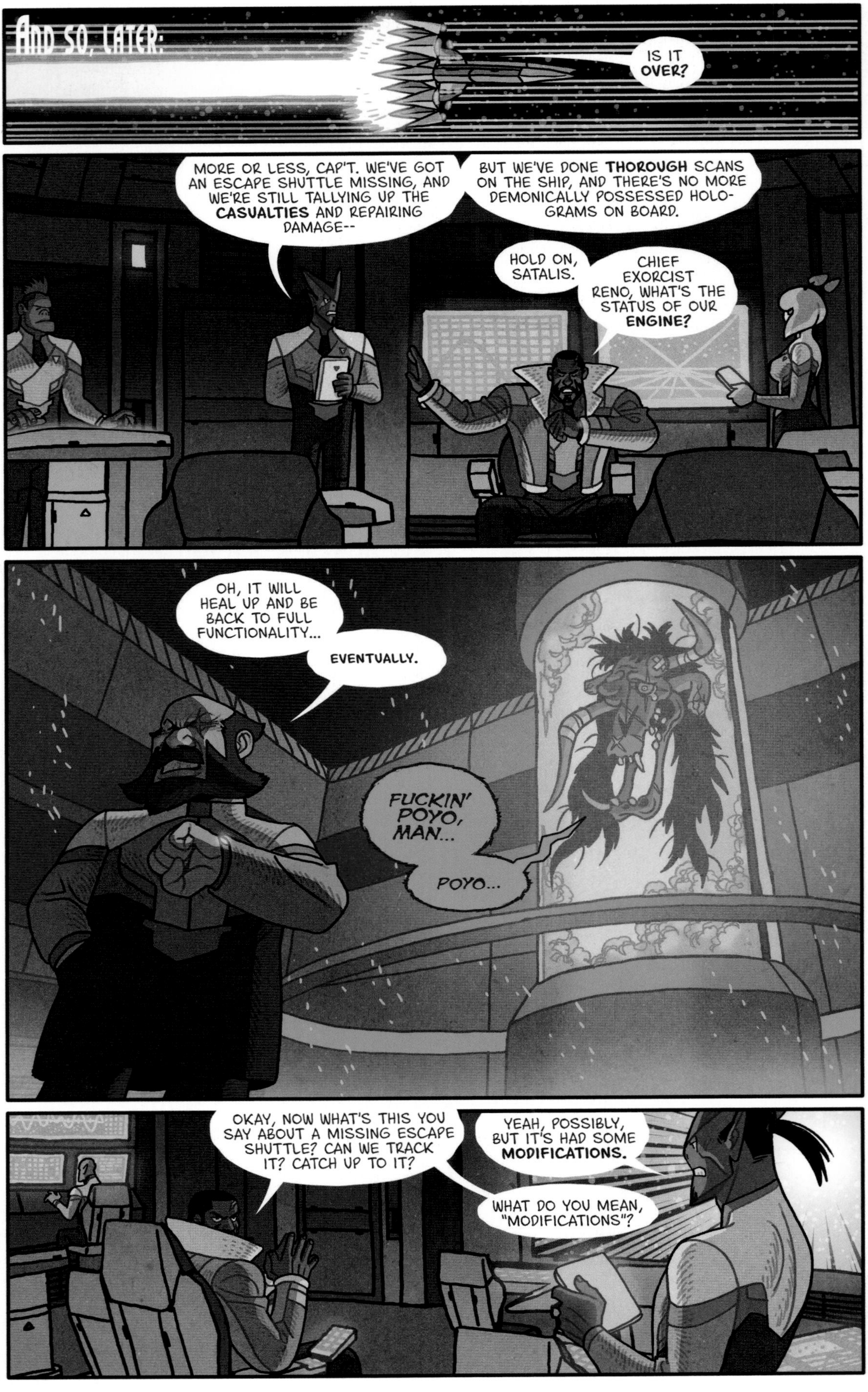

AND SO, LATER:
IS IT OVER?
MORE OR LESS, CAP'T. WE'VE GOT AN ESCAPE SHUTTLE MISSING, AND WE'RE STILL TALLYING UP THE CASUALTIES AND REPAIRING DAMAGE--
BUT WE'VE DONE THOROUGH SCANS ON THE SHIP, AND THERE'S NO MORE DEMONICALLY POSSESSED HOLOGRAMS ON BOARD.
HOLD ON, SATALIS.
CHIEF EXORCIST RENO, WHAT'S THE STATUS OF OUR ENGINE?
OH, IT WILL HEAL UP AND BE BACK TO FULL FUNCTIONALITY...
EVENTUALLY.
FUCKIN' POYO, MAN...
POYO...
OKAY, NOW WHAT'S THIS YOU SAY ABOUT A MISSING ESCAPE SHUTTLE? CAN WE TRACK IT? CATCH UP TO IT?
YEAH, POSSIBLY, BUT IT'S HAD SOME MODIFICATIONS.
WHAT DO YOU MEAN, "MODIFICATIONS"?

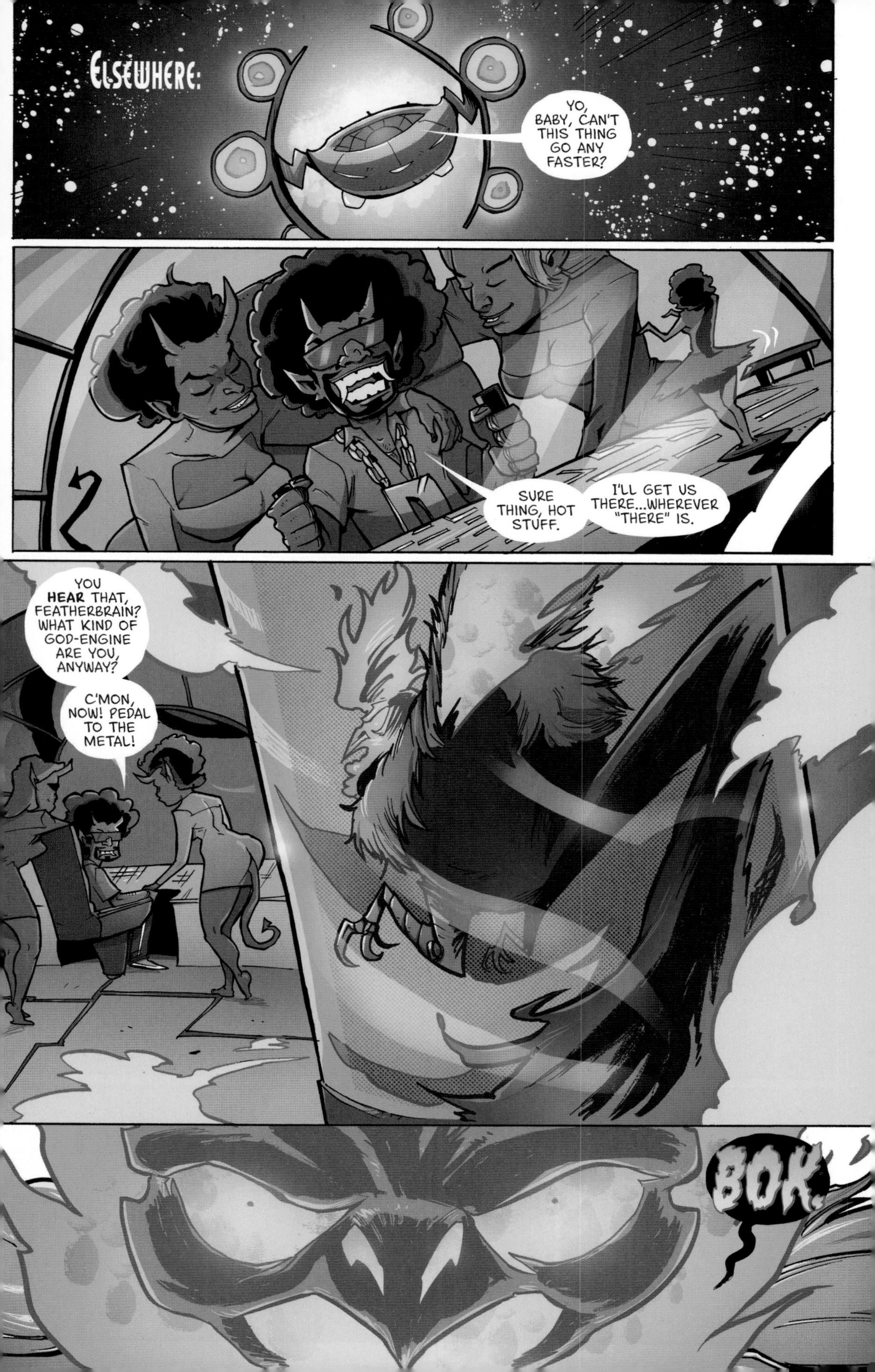
ELSEWHERE:
YO, BABY, CAN'T THIS THING GO ANY FASTER?
SURE THING, HOT STUFF.
I'LL GET US THERE...WHEREVER "THERE" IS.
YOU **HEAR** THAT, FEATHERBRAIN? WHAT KIND OF GOD-ENGINE ARE YOU, ANYWAY?
C'MON, NOW! PEDAL TO THE METAL!
BOK.

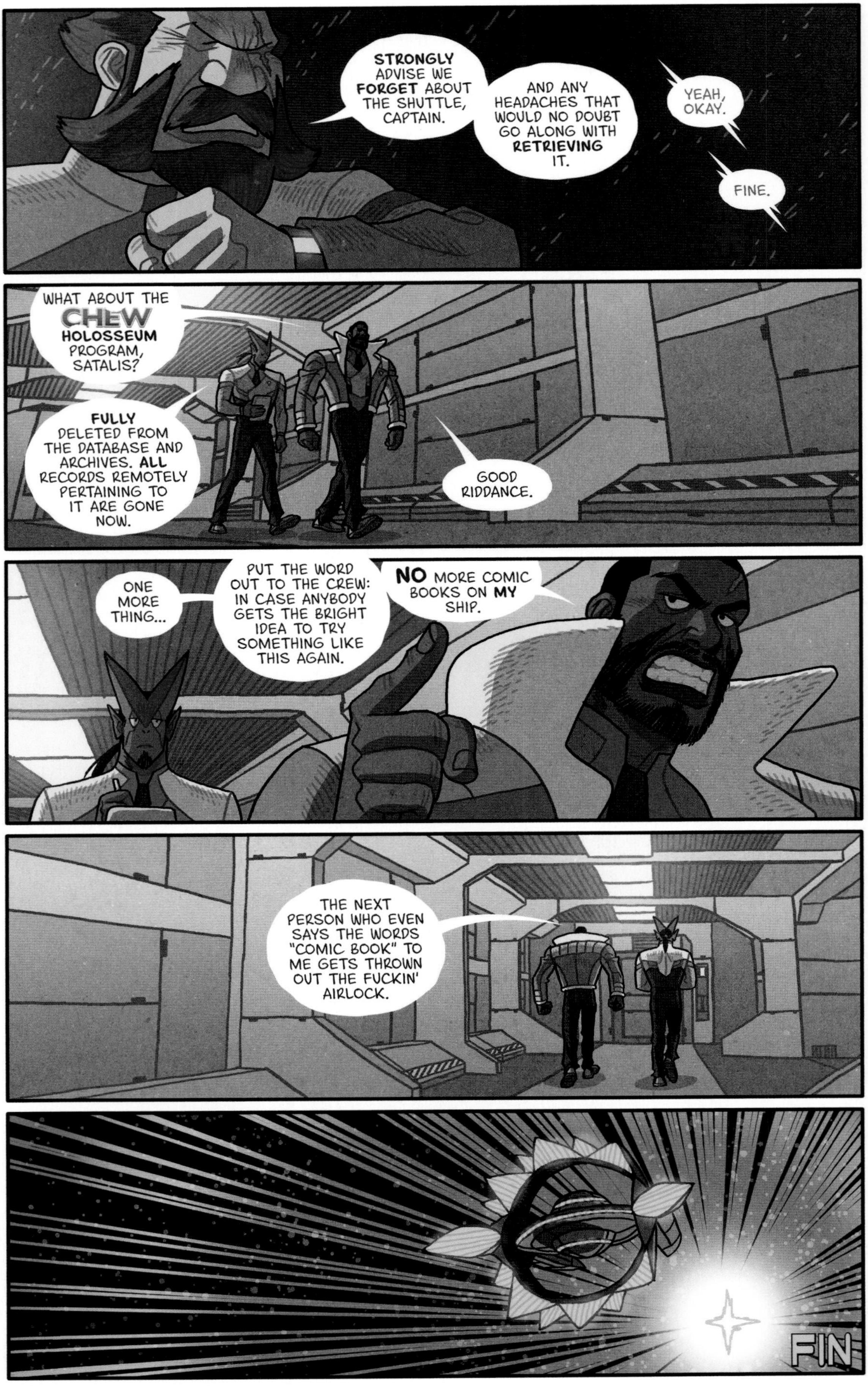
STRONGLY ADVISE WE FORGET ABOUT THE SHUTTLE, CAPTAIN.
AND ANY HEADACHES THAT WOULD NO DOUBT GO ALONG WITH RETRIEVING IT.
YEAH, OKAY.
FINE.
WHAT ABOUT THE CHEW HOLOSSEUM PROGRAM, SATALIS?
FULLY DELETED FROM THE DATABASE AND ARCHIVES. ALL RECORDS REMOTELY PERTAINING TO IT ARE GONE NOW.
GOOD RIDDANCE.
ONE MORE THING...
PUT THE WORD OUT TO THE CREW: IN CASE ANYBODY GETS THE BRIGHT IDEA TO TRY SOMETHING LIKE THIS AGAIN.
NO MORE COMIC BOOKS ON MY SHIP.
THE NEXT PERSON WHO EVEN SAYS THE WORDS "COMIC BOOK" TO ME GETS THROWN OUT THE FUCKIN' AIRLOCK.
FIN

COVER GALLERY

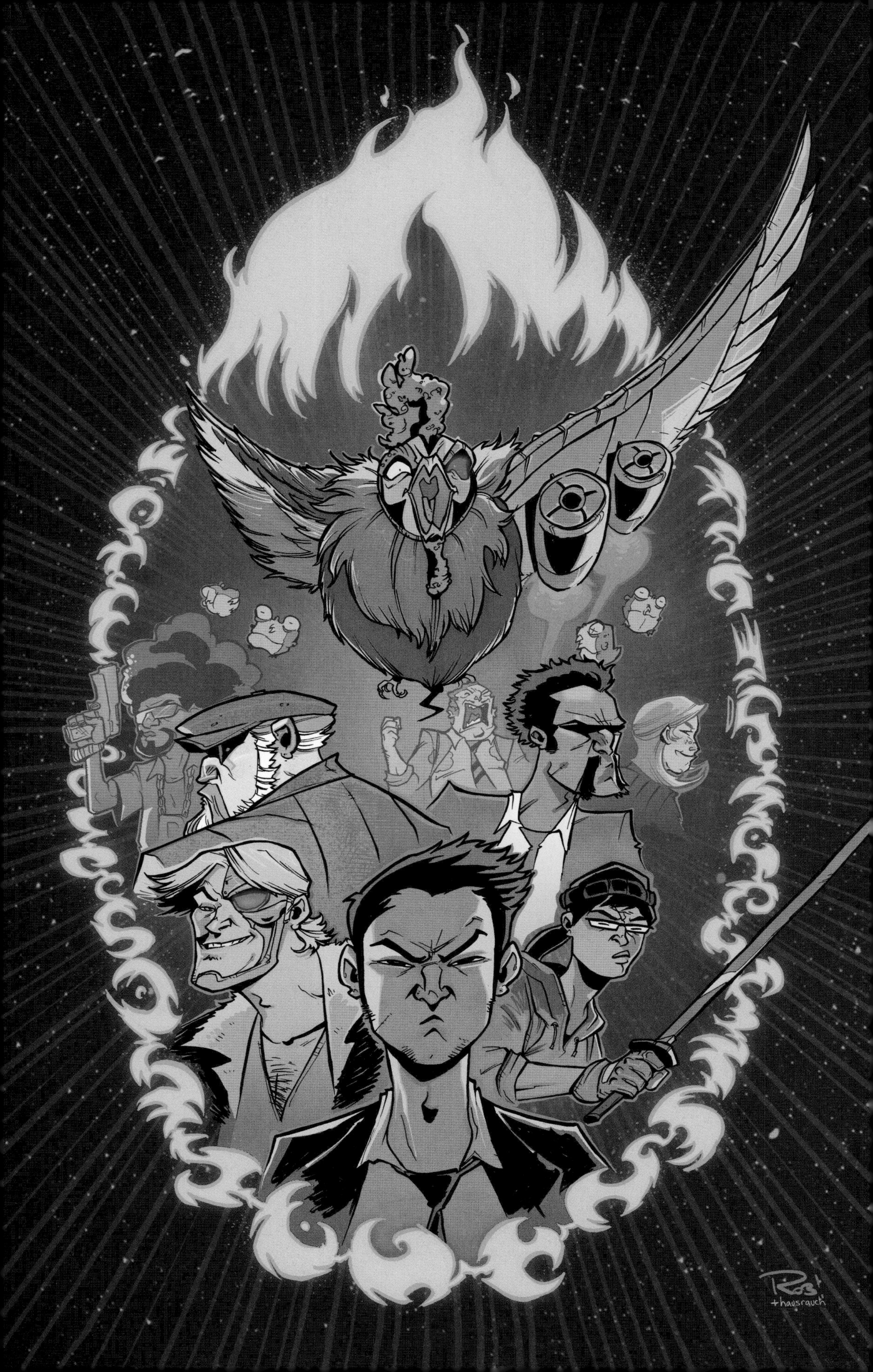
Ros
+hausrauch

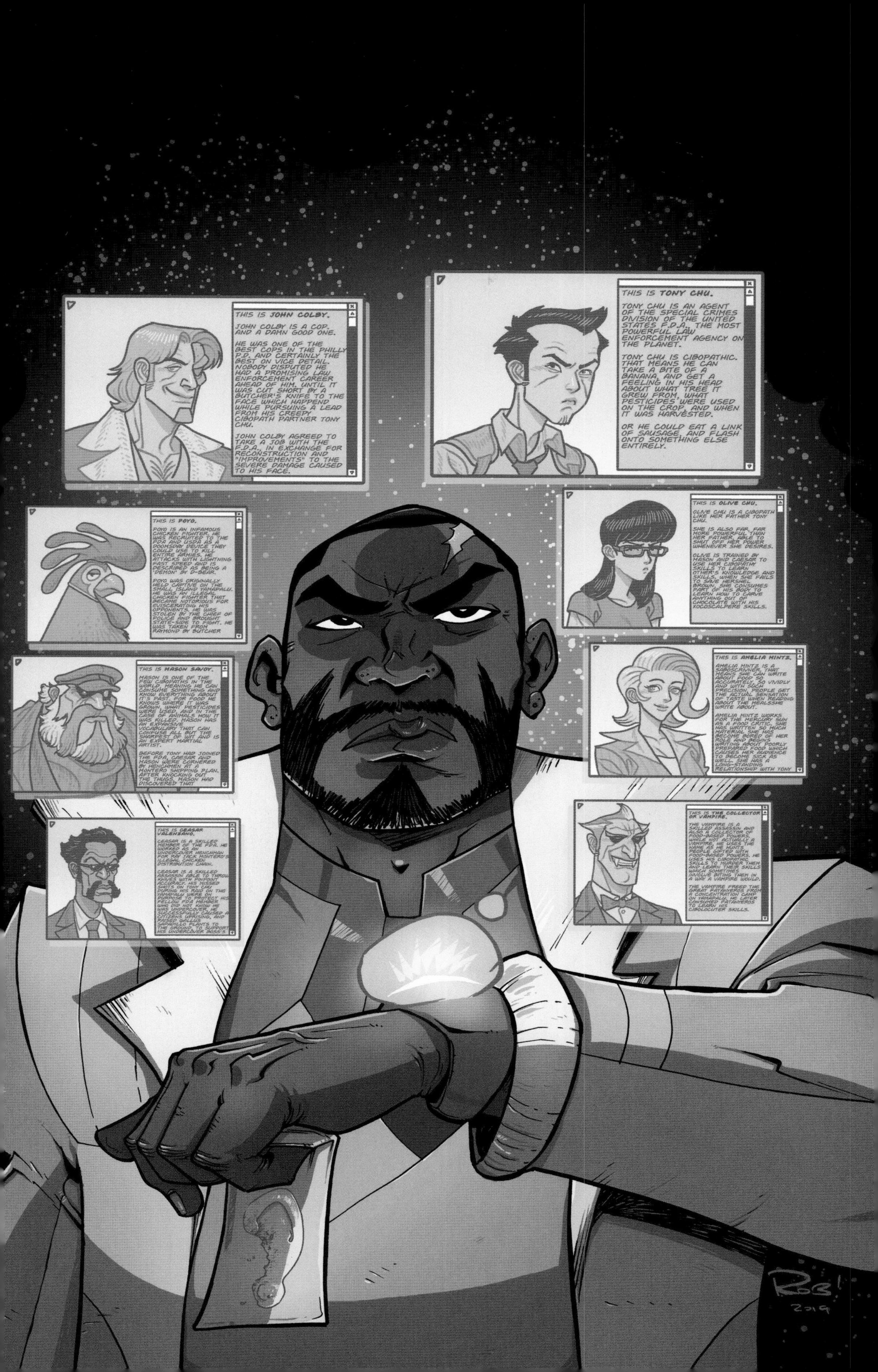

THIS IS JOHN COLBY.
JOHN COLBY IS A COP. AND A DAMN GOOD ONE.
HE WAS ONE OF THE BEST COPS IN THE PHILLY P.D. AND CERTAINLY THE BEST ON VICE DETAIL. NOBODY DISPUTED HE HAD A PROMISING LAW ENFORCEMENT CAREER AHEAD OF HIM. UNTIL IT WAS CUT SHORT BY A BUTCHER'S KNIFE TO THE FACE WHICH HAPPEND WHILE PURSUING A LEAD FROM HIS CREEPY CIBOPATH PARTNER TONY CHU.
JOHN COLBY AGREED TO TAKE A JOB WITH THE F.D.A., IN EXCHANGE FOR RECONSTRUCTION AND "IMPROVEMENTS" TO THE SEVERE DAMAGE CAUSED TO HIS FACE.
THIS IS TONY CHU.
TONY CHU IS AN AGENT OF THE SPECIAL CRIMES DIVISION OF THE UNITED STATES F.D.A., THE MOST POWERFUL LAW ENFORCEMENT AGENCY ON THE PLANET.
TONY CHU IS CIBOPATHIC. THAT MEANS HE CAN TAKE A BITE OF A BANANA, AND GET A FEELING IN HIS HEAD ABOUT WHAT TREE IT GREW FROM, WHAT PESTICIDES WERE USED ON THE CROP, AND WHEN IT WAS HARVESTED.
OR HE COULD EAT A LINK OF SAUSAGE, AND FLASH ONTO SOMETHING ELSE ENTIRELY.
THIS IS POYO.
POYO IS AN INFAMOUS CHICKEN FIGHTER. HE WAS RECRUITED TO THE FDA AND USDA AS A DOOMSDAY DEVICE THEY COULD USE TO KILL ENTIRE ARMIES. HE ATTACKS WITH LIGHTNING FAST SPEED AND IS DESCRIBED AS BEING A 'DEMON' BY D-BEAR.
POYO WAS ORIGINALLY HELD CAPTIVE ON THE SMALL ISLAND YAMAPALU. HE WAS AN ILLEGAL CHICKEN FIGHTER THAT BECAME NOTORIOUS FOR EVISCERATING HIS OPPONENTS. HE WAS STOLEN BY THE CHIEF OF POLICE AND BROUGHT STATE-SIDE TO FIGHT. HE WAS TAKEN FROM RAYMOND BY BUTCHER
THIS IS OLIVE CHU.
OLIVE CHU IS A CIBOPATH LIKE HER FATHER TONY CHU.
SHE IS ALSO FAR, FAR MORE POWERFUL THAN HER FATHER, ABLE TO SHUT OFF HER POWER WHENEVER SHE DESIRES.
OLIVE IS TRAINED BY MASON AND CAESAR TO USE HER CIBOPATHY SKILLS TO LEARN OTHER'S KNOWLEDGE AND SKILLS. WHEN SHE FAILS TO SAVE HERSHEL BROWN, SHE CONSUMES PART OF HIS BODY TO LEARN HOW TO CARVE ANYTHING OUT OF CHOCOLATE WITH HIS XOCOSCALPERE SKILLS.
THIS IS MASON SAVOY.
MASON IS ONE OF THE FEW CIBOPATHS IN THE WORLD, MEANING HE CAN CONSUME SOMETHING AND KNOW EVERYTHING ABOUT IT'S PAST. FOR FOOD HE KNOWS WHERE IT WAS GROWN, WHAT PESTICIDES WERE USED, AND IN THE CASE OF ANIMALS HOW IT WAS KILLED. MASON HAS AN EXPANSIVE VOCABULARY THAT CAN CONFUSE ALL BUT THE SHARPEST OF WIT AND IS AN EXPERT MARTIAL ARTIST.
BEFORE TONY HAD JOINED THE FDA, CAESAR AND MASON WERE CORNERED BY HENCHMEN AT A MONTERO SHIPPING PLAN. AFTER KNOCKING OUT THE THUGS, MASON HAD DISCOVERED THAT
THIS IS AMELIA MINTZ.
AMELIA MINTZ IS A SABOSCRIVNER. THAT MEANS SHE CAN WRITE ABOUT FOOD SO ACCURATELY, SO VIVIDLY AND WITH SUCH PRECISION, PEOPLE GET THE ACTUAL SENSATION OF TASTE WHEN READING ABOUT THE MEALSSHE WRITE ABOUT.
AMELIA MINTZ WORKS FOR THE MERCURY SUN AS A FOOD CRITIC. SHE HAS WRITTEN SO MUCH MATERIAL SHE HAS BECOME BORED OF HER ROLE AND BEGINS WRITING ABOUT POORLY PREPARED FOOD WHICH CAUSES HER AUDIENCE TO BECOME SICK AS WELL. SHE HAS A LONG-STANDING RELATIONSHIP WITH TONY
THIS IS CEASAR VALENZANO.
CEASAR IS A SKILLED MEMBER OF THE FDA. HE WORKED AS AN UNDERCOVER HENCHMAN FOR RAY JACK MONTERO'S ILLEGAL CHICKEN DISTRIBUTION CHAIN.
CEASAR IS A SKILLED ASSASSIN ABLE TO THROW KNIVES WITH PINPOINT ACCURACY. HIS MISSED SHOTS ON TONY CHU DURING HIS RAID ON THE YAMAPALU WERE ON PURPOSE TO PROTECT HIS FELLOW FDA MEMBER WHO DID NOT KNOW HE WAS UNDERCOVER. HE SUCCESSFULLY CAUSED A CITIZENS UPRISING, AND RAISED GALLUS SAPADILLO PLANTS TO THE GROUND, TO SUPPORT HIS UNDERCOVER BOSS'S
THIS IS THE COLLECTOR OR VAMPIRE.
THE VAMPIRE IS A SKILLED ASSASSIN AND ALSO A COLLECTOR OF FOOD-BASED POWERS. WHILE NOT ACTUALLY A VAMPIRE, HE USES THE NAME AS HE HUNTS PEOPLE GIFTED WITH FOOD-BASED POWERS. HE USES HIS CIBOPATHIC SKILLS TO MURDER THEM AND LEARN THEIR SKILLS WHICH SOMETIMES INVOLVE BITING THEM IN A WAY A VAMPIRE WOULD.
THE VAMPIRE FREED THE GREAT FATANYEROS FROM A CONCENTRATION CAMP ON YAMAPALU. HE LATER CONSUMED FATANYEROS TO LEARN HIS CIBOLOCUTER SKILLS.
ROB! 2019

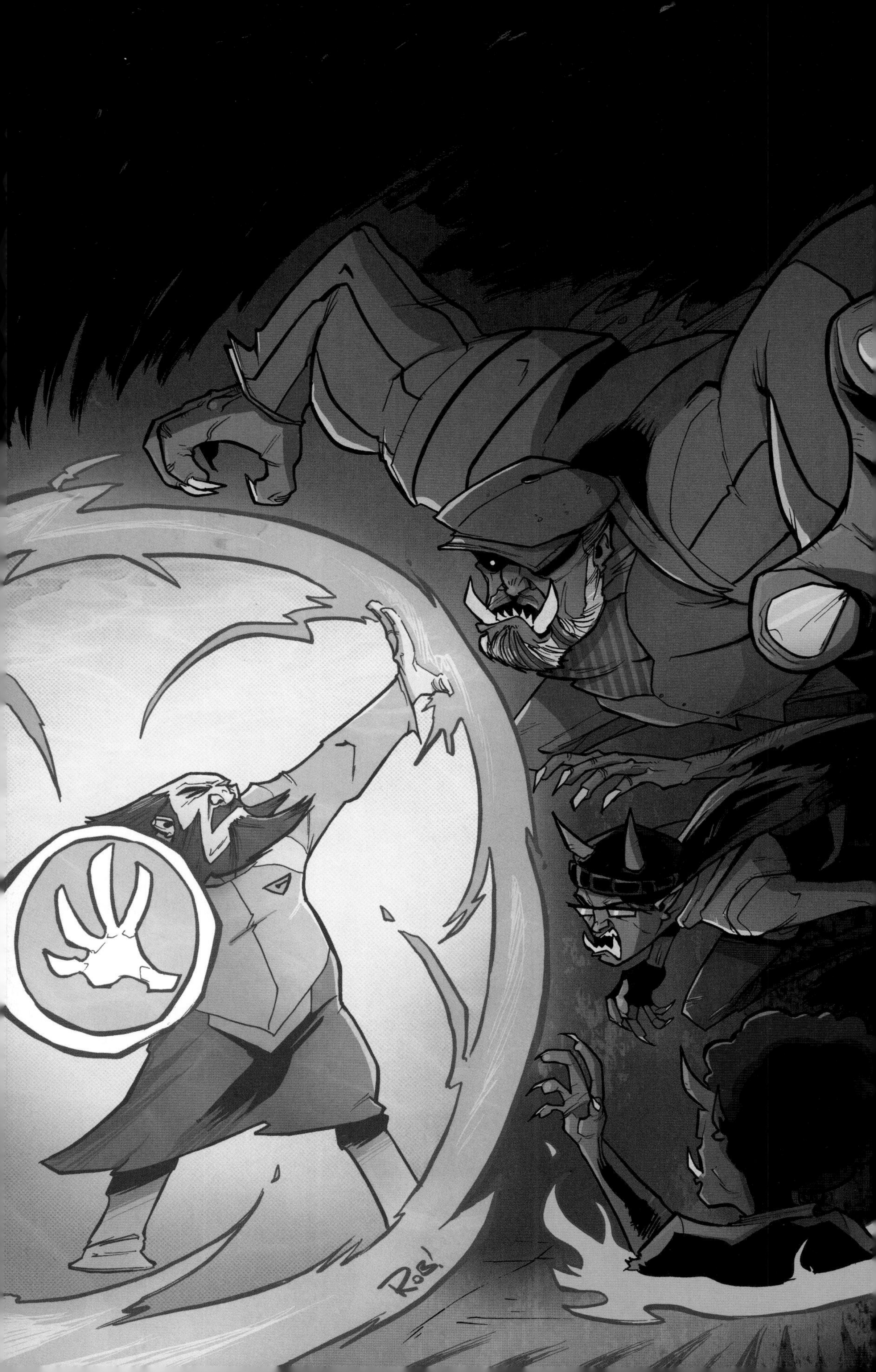
ROB!

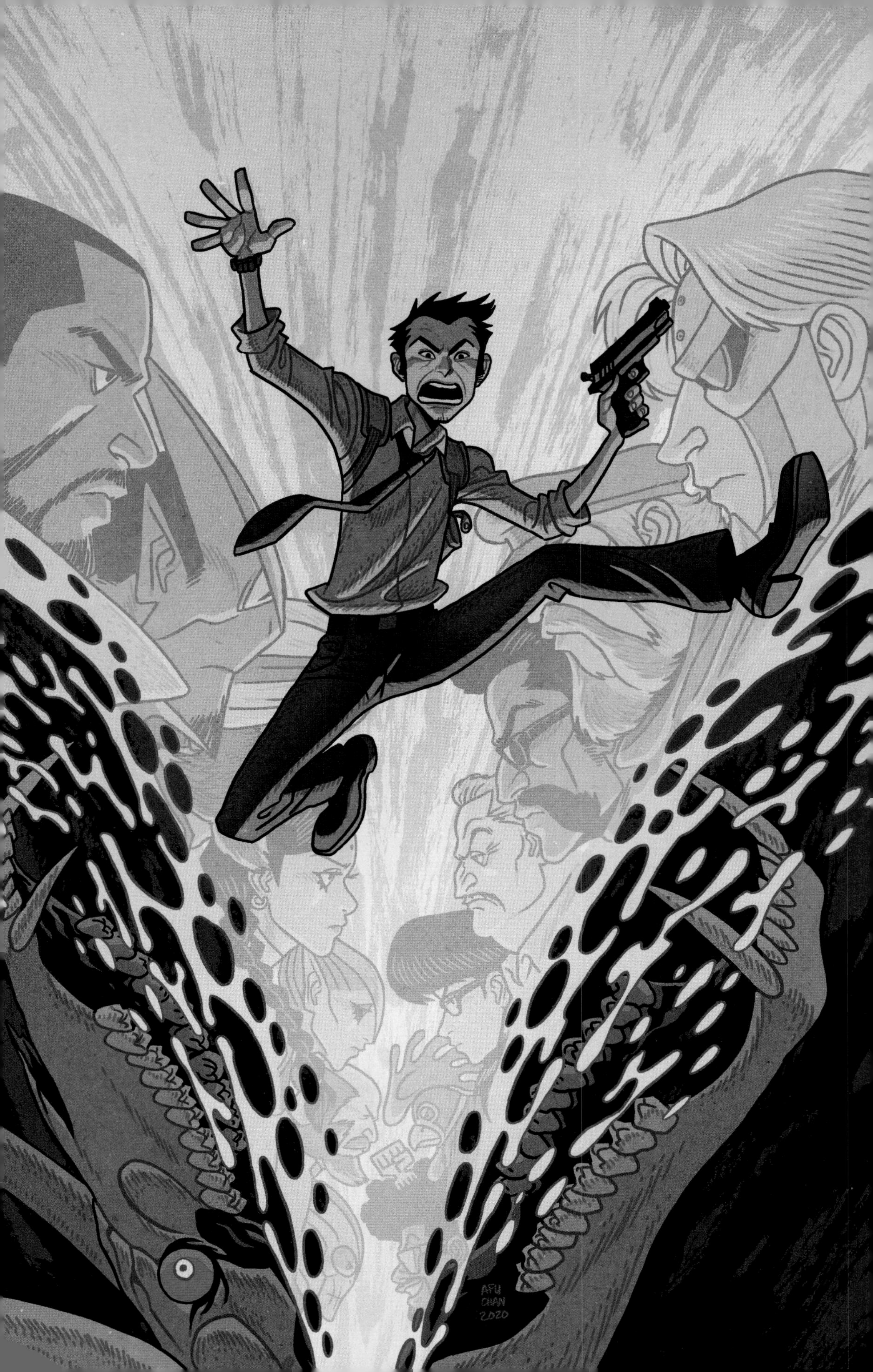
AFU
CHAN
2020

CHARON PERSONNEL &

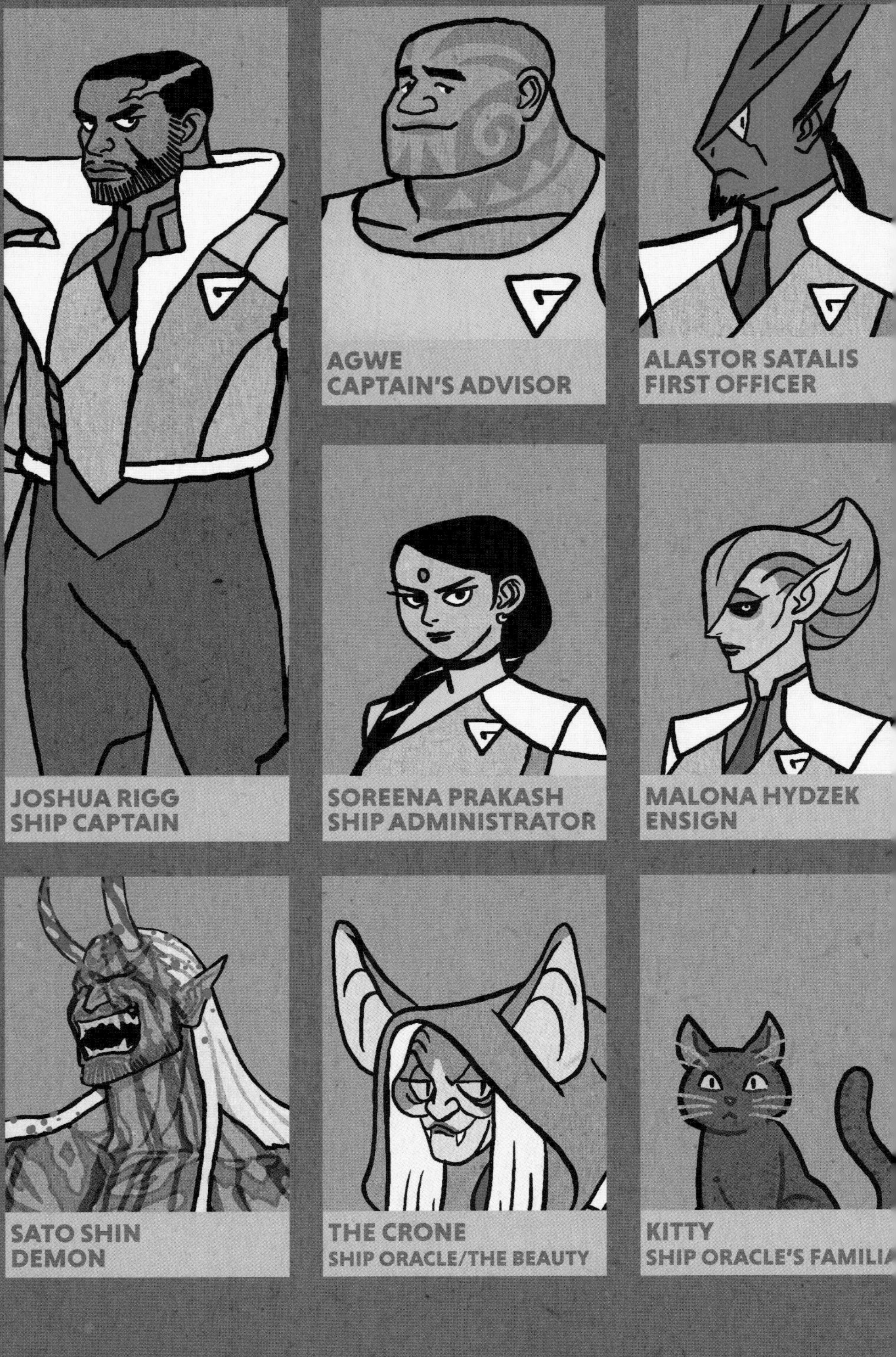
JOSHUA RIGG
SHIP CAPTAIN
AGWE
CAPTAIN'S ADVISOR
ALASTOR SATALIS
FIRST OFFICER
SOREENA PRAKASH
SHIP ADMINISTRATOR
MALONA HYDZEK
ENSIGN
SATO SHIN
DEMON
THE CRONE
SHIP ORACLE/THE BEAUTY
KITTY
SHIP ORACLE'S FAMILIA

COMBATANT RECORD

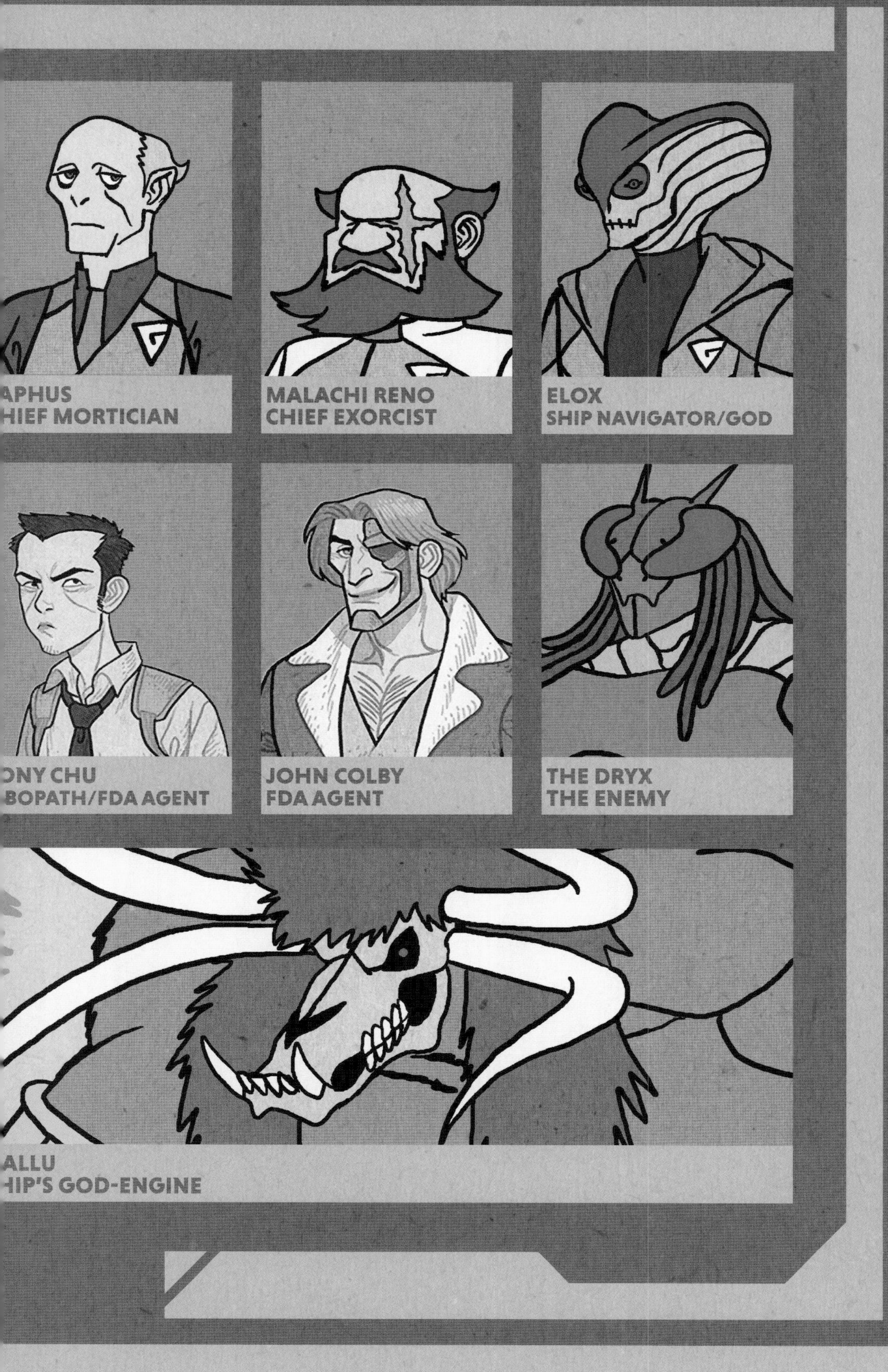
APHUS
HIEF MORTICIAN
MALACHI RENO
CHIEF EXORCIST
ELOX
SHIP NAVIGATOR/GOD
ONY CHU
BOPATH/FDA AGENT
JOHN COLBY
FDA AGENT
THE DRYX
THE ENEMY
ALLU
HIP'S GOD-ENGINE

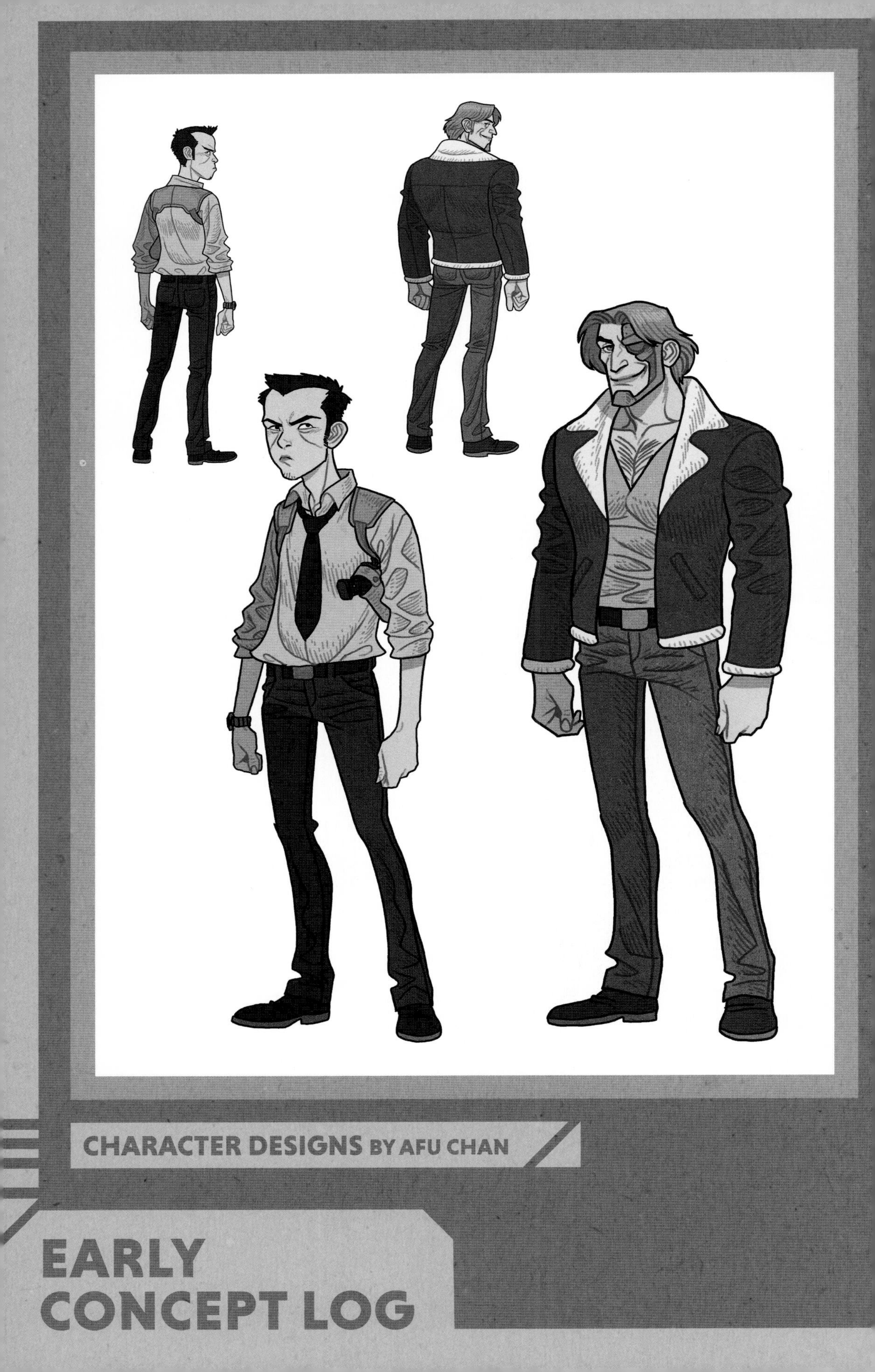

CHARACTER DESIGNS BY AFU CHAN

EARLY CONCEPT LOG

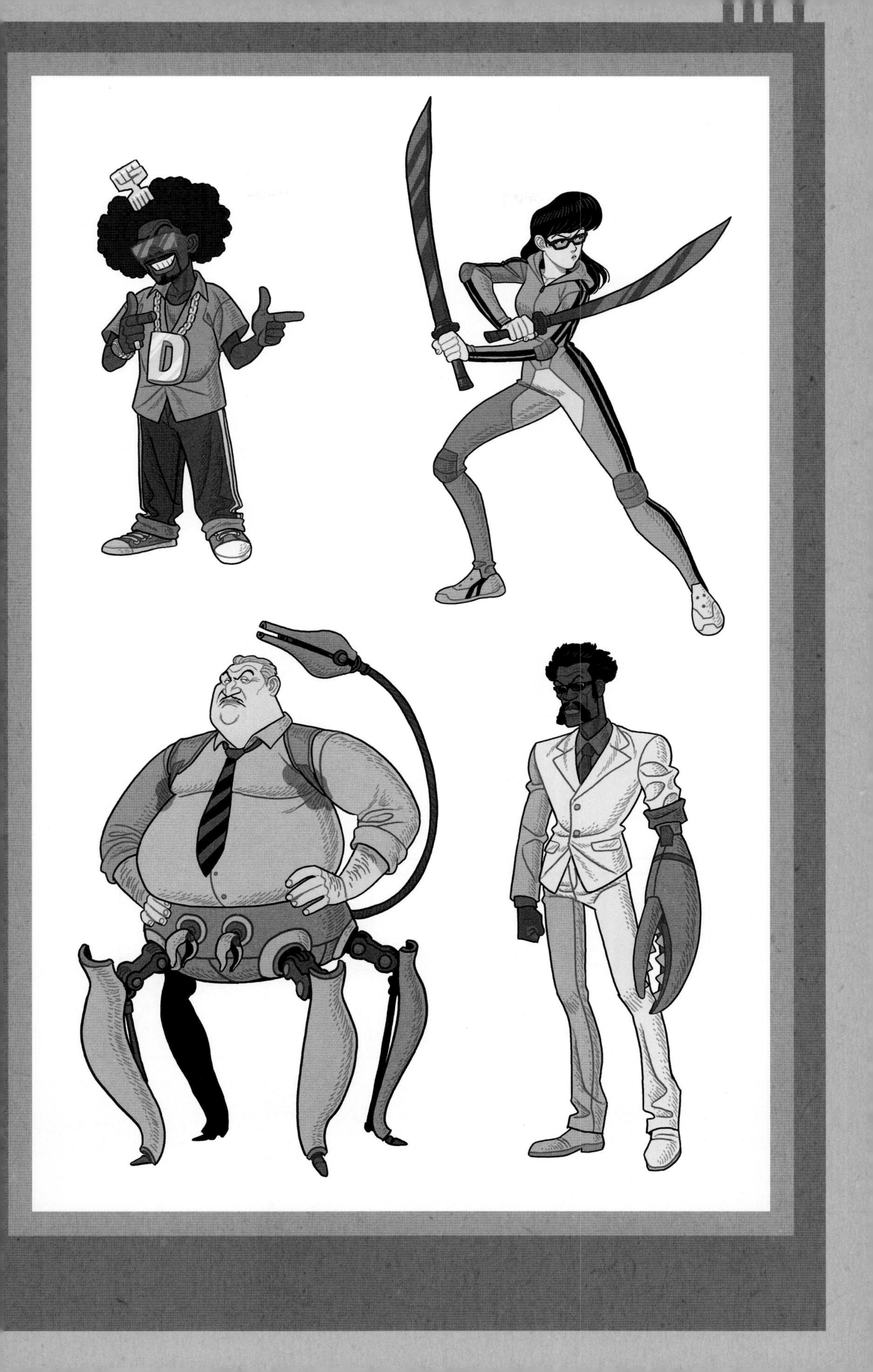
D

AW, GODDAMMIT, TONY.
YOU BETTER DO YOUR EXORCISM STUFF PRONTO, SHORTY.
NOT SURE HOW MUCH LONGER I'M GONNA LAST BEFO--
BEFORE I

ISSUE #3 THUMBNAILS

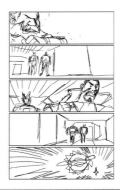

EARLY CONCEPT LOG

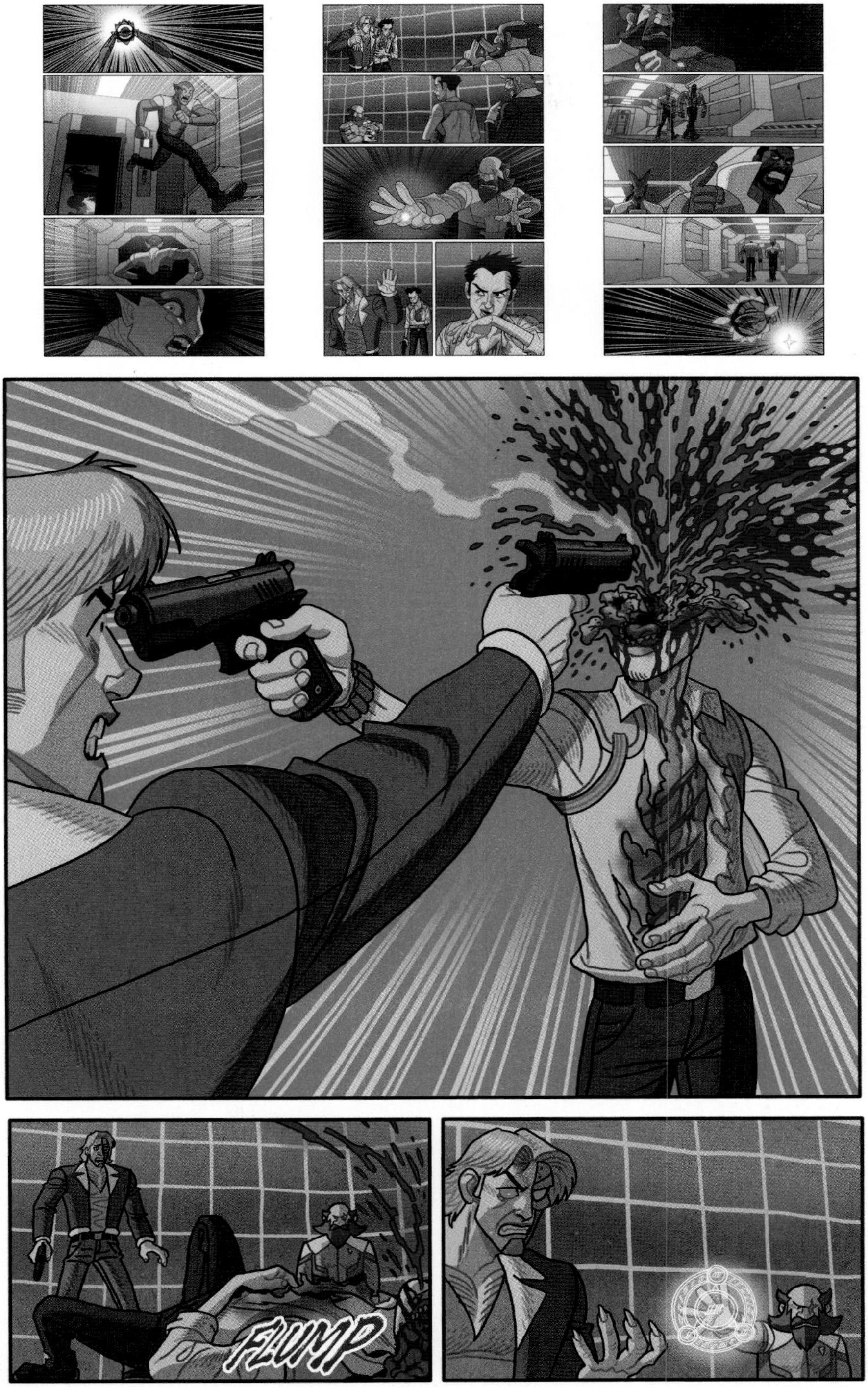
FLUMP

ISSUE #3 COLOR PASS

FOR MORE TALES FROM ROBERT KIRKMAN AND SKYBOUND

ROBERT KIRKMAN
LORENZO DE FELICI
ANNALISA LEONI
OBLIVION SONG
CHAPTER FOUR

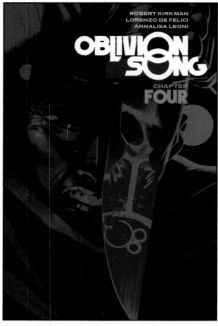

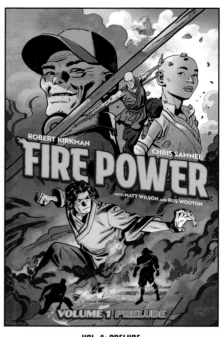

CHAPTER ONE
ISBN: 978-1-5343-0642-4
$9.99

CHAPTER TWO
ISBN: 978-1-5343-1057-5
$16.99

CHAPTER THREE
ISBN: 978-1-5343-1057-5
$16.99

CHAPTER FOUR
ISBN: 978-1-5343-1517-4
$16.99

ROBERT KIRKMAN
CHRIS SAMNEE
FIRE POWER
WITH MATT WILSON AND RUS WOOTON
VOLUME 1 PRELUDE

VOL. 1: PRELUDE
ISBN: 978-1-5343-1655-3
$9.99

EXCELLENCE
VOLUME ONE
KILL THE PAST

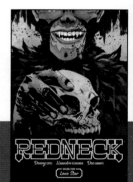

VOL. 1: KILL THE PAST TP
ISBN: 978-1-5343-1362-0
$16.99

MANIFEST DESTINY

VOL. 1: FLORA & FAUNA TP
ISBN: 978-1-60706-982-9
$9.99

VOL. 2: AMPHIBIA & INSECTA TP
ISBN: 978-1-63215-052-3
$14.99

VOL. 3: CHIROPTERA & CARNIFORMAVES TP
ISBN: 978-1-63215-397-5
$14.99

VOL. 4: SASQUATCH TP
ISBN: 978-1-63215-890-1
$14.99

VOL. 5: MNEMOPHOBIA & CHRONOPHOBIA TP
ISBN: 978-1-5343-0230-3
$16.99

VOL. 6: FORTIS & INVISIBILIA TP
ISBN: 978-1-5343-0513-7
$16.99

VOL. 7: TALPA LUMBRICUS & LEPUS TP
ISBN: 978-1-5343-1589-1
$16.99

BY KIRKMAN & AZACETA
OUTCAST

VOL. 1: A DARKNESS SURROUNDS HIM TP
ISBN: 978-1-63215-053-0
$9.99

VOL. 2: A VAST AND UNENDING RUIN TP
ISBN: 978-1-63215-448-4
$14.99

VOL. 3: THIS LITTLE LIGHT TP
ISBN: 978-1-63215-693-8
$14.99

VOL. 4: UNDER DEVIL'S WING TP
ISBN: 978-1-5343-0050-7
$14.99

VOL. 5: THE NEW PATH TP
ISBN: 978-1-5343-0249-5
$16.99

VOL. 6: INVASION TP
ISBN: 978-1-5343-0751-3
$16.99

VOL. 7: THE DARKNESS GROWS TP
ISBN: 978-1-5343-1239-5
$16.99

REDNECK
Lone Star

VOL. 1: DEEP IN THE HEART TP
ISBN: 978-1-5343-0331-7
$16.99

VOL. 2: THE EYES UPON YOU TP
ISBN: 978-1-5343-0665-3
$16.99

VOL. 3: LONGHORNS TP
ISBN: 978-1-5343-1050-6
$16.99

VOL. 4: LONE STAR TP
ISBN: 978-1-5343-1367-5
$16.99